THE HEARTBREAKER'S WIFE

SMALL TOWN BACHELORS

SUSAN WARNER

EG PUBLISHING

THE HEARTBREAKER'S WIFE

First Edition. January 29, 2023.

Copyright © 2023 EG Publishing

Written by Susan Warner.

If you like to get a free book from Susan Warner and would like to join her Newsletter sign up here Susan's newsletter

CHAPTER 1

"Kathy, let's try again."

Kathy Ellis knew the therapist was only trying to do her best by her. In fact, if Kathy were honest, she would say that Dr. Talls had gotten the furthest with her. As she lay on the couch in the living room, she found herself in a calmer state than she had been before—calm enough to know that she wasn't sure if she wanted to consider having a relationship with another man. She had her brother, and he was the only person she could count on.

Being orphaned was one thing, but being separated from her birth brother for most of her teenage years had taught her not to rely on anything or anyone. Reid Chance, her brother, had come to find her, and that spoke to his sense of obligation. Reid was a good man, but even good men had to be able to live their lives and find love. Reid had found love with Gloria Danvers. When people fell in love, everything changed. They went from faithful to forgetful.

"Kathy, are you with me?"

Kathy finally opened her eyes and smiled at the doctor.

"I'm here, Dr. Talls."

"What are you thinking?"

Kathy thought to herself that the doctor didn't want to know what she was really thinking. She was thinking about the man who might be a problem to her brother's happiness—Jack. Jack Danvers was his name, and he was Gloria Denver's brother. What kind of name was Jack anyway? Jack thought his good looks would get him everywhere. He must have been six-three with a square jaw that begged for a woman's hand to caress it. He was a solid man whom she would have expected to see in a fairy tale rather than running a food cart in a park. Jack was a whole bunch of contradictions.

"Kathy?"

"I'm sorry. I was just thinking that I feel like I owe Reid."

"He's your brother."

"Yes, he is, but that doesn't mean that I don't owe him."

"In most families, they don't owe one another. What they do for one another is because they love one another."

Kathy didn't look at the doctor. She couldn't bring herself to look at Dr. Talls and not reveal what she thought about doctors. She was never good about hiding her thoughts from her face. Now it wouldn't be any different.

"Kathy, I feel like you aren't really here today. Is there something you want to talk about?"

"No, I think that I've had a lot of things to go over in my mind lately, especially your thoughts on how families are supposed to interact. I think we need to wrap up this session a little earlier today. "

"Of course, knowing your limits is as important as knowing when it's time to take a step back from the events as well."

Kathy smiled and knew this was going to be the last session she had with Dr. Talls. Kathy had been planning to leave for quite some time. She wasn't going to wait for Reid to throw her out or decide he didn't have room for her now that he had found love. She was determined to leave in her own time and on her own terms. She wouldn't have the last memory of them be her begging to stay. The doctor wouldn't understand that, so there was no point in telling her the plan.

Then Kathy heard the music that the doctor turned on when the session ended, and it took all she has in her not to moan out loud.

"Doctor, really? Let's not do the music today. I think we've done enough with polite rituals," Kathy said as she sat up and looked at the doctor. The doctor had the same concerned motherly look on her face that she'd had all along, and now what was once comforting had become something that sparked some anger in Kathy. So many people tried to help when they didn't understand the problem. Love was fickle, and Kathy was damaged. Oh, it wasn't the damage you could see on the outside. It was the damage that emotionally seeped out of you and made every relationship toxic.

The doctor quietly packed up her bag and belongings, knowing automatically that this wasn't the time to push for explanations. Kathy felt terrible at first. Then as she was guiding the doctor out the door and saying all the polite pleasantries, she saw the picture of Gloria and her brother Jack standing next to one another. His arm was around Gloria, and then it became clear that Jack would always be in the picture if left to his own devices.

Dependable Jack, always there to hold Gloria's hand. Jack didn't need to be there anymore; Reid was. After the doctor left, the first thing Kathy did was call her brother, Reid.

"Hey, what are you doing today?" For a moment, Kathy didn't hear anything but a large sigh. "Reid?"

"Kathy, sorry," he said in a low tone that seemed restless.

"What's up?"

"What's up? I can't just call my brother?"

"I'm sorry, Kathy. I'm not in a great mood, and you are the only one who's called me today."

"Okay, what's the issue?" He didn't answer, but Kathy knew Reid. The longer it took for him to answer, the deeper the problem.

"There's nothing. I mean, I know there's nothing, so it doesn't matter."

"Reid, really?"

"Okay. It's her brother."

Kathy didn't even have to hear the rest of the story to know it was true. It was Jack's fault.

"Mr. 'All Smiles While He's Blocking Out The Sun.'"

"I don't think he blocks out the sun," Reid grumbles.

"Well, let's agree to disagree on what kind of bully person he is. Why don't you tell me what the problem is so we can go on from there?"

"They are planning on their time together to remember their dad."

"Remember their dad?" Kathy asked.

"Yes, they have a tradition that on the day their father was lost at sea, they spend it together. She told me they were spending the time, so it wasn't a surprise. The thing is that I know her father played a large part in their lives, and when I asked if she wanted me to drive her to the restaurant or pick a place that might work for us three, she seemed like she wasn't sure she wanted me to go at all."

Kathy was automatically upset because Reid wasn't happy.

"What is it? Do you want them not to go?" Kathy hoped that Reid wasn't jealous of Jack because that would be a larger problem with the relationship.

"No, I do want them to go, but there's no part of my life that I haven't invited Gloria into, and I guess I just have to wait to be invited into this part of her life. It caught me unaware, and it hurts. I mean, it's her brother, so it shouldn't hurt or even be an issue."

"Oh!" Kathy said, turning to look at the photo and knowing that this had to be dealt with. "So, what do you want to do about it?" Kathy heard the deep sigh on the other line.

"There's nothing to do. We've spoken about it, and she says she knows that it's something she needs to work on."

"She's being open and honest with you. That's more than a lot of couples have these days," Kathy said as she nonchalantly walked about the room. The room was filled with the things she and Reid had put in it. Each object was a fond memory. Now she looked upon the relics and tried to decide which ones she would take with her.

After fielding more questions on how the business was and how the horses on Reid's therapy ranch were doing, Kathy hung up the phone, determined now more than ever to help her brother.

Kathy went to her computer to do some invoices. Doing some busy work would help get her mind off of the problem known as Jack as well give her some space to think over the issue in a calm fashion. Instead, the first invoice she ran into was one for Jack Danvers and the Claw House delivery Gloria and Reid had done for a fundraising event for Grayson. Kathy looked at the invoice and then the amount that Reid wanted to tip and knew that Jack must have a great product because Reid didn't let family get in the way of money.

Kathy held the invoice in her hand and thought about delivering the money herself. She could always say she was going to visit Reid, and it was on her way, like literally. Reid was a big boy, and he didn't need his sister butting into his life. Even though it did seem like Reid thought his hands were tied in dealing with Jack.

Kathy twirled the invoice in her hand and then decided that just dropping the invoice wasn't really interfering. She was taking in the lay of the land, was all. Even Kathy had to snort at her musings. She wasn't going to take in the land. She was going to give Jack a firm talking to about how the landscape had changed.

Maybe ten minutes had passed, and Kathy had figured out her itinerary when she was in Inheritance Bay. It would be nice to see the twins, Grayson and Rose. The other interesting, not interesting, thing that was on Kathy's mind was their brother, Quinn.

Quinn was a unique man, related or not. He had a way of just being silent and still, and then everyone would tell him everything. Kathy shook her head and tried to think of ways she wouldn't have to engage face-to-face with him. She had been delirious once after getting a root canal and had taken some painkillers that didn't knock her out soon enough. It was long enough for her to start blabbing about how she would leave Reid's life when he found love.

Kathy nodded as the memory came back to her. She should be doing exactly what she had said all those days before to Quinn. Kathy felt as though it was time to move on for Reid's sake. She could just do a small drive by Jack's and give him a head's up about where his new place was going to be, and then she could move on. It was the least she could do for Reid. During the time Kathy had been lost, she had always dreamed that someone would save her. When Reid showed up, she promised not to ruin what he had by overstaying her welcome. Kathy had tons of memories to hold on to. Reid had been there to help her through college. Reid had been there as her support when she decided to try her hand at business. There was no endeavor that she tried that he didn't support her and encourage her.

It was very clear to her what needed to happen. As she recalled all of the times that Reid had been there for her, she couldn't imagine not doing something for him when it seemed that he needed it most. She picked up her phone and went into her bedroom to pack a bag. She was going to pay Jack Danvers a visit that was long overdue. When she left, she was going to make sure that Jack Danvers wasn't an issue any longer.

CHAPTER 2

*J*ack gave the machine another look, and then stood back, inspecting the gleaming metal surface and the plastic cylinder that protruded from the floor. It wasn't much to look at to the naked eye. Jack knew that in the grand scheme of life, it probably wasn't that all of a big deal to anyone else but those who needed it.

To a passerby, it was a circular wooden base that had a plastic cylinder poking from the middle. The cylinder was see-through and was wide enough to be hollow. Next to the base was a tube that fed from the tube to a dog bowl that was on the side. Jack looked at the simple contraption and knew this was it. Oh, he had said that before, but now he was sure he had it.

This was going to do the trick, and he had gotten the answer by sticking to his guns.

A knock on his garage door made him roll his eyes as well as look at his new project longingly. Some people would consider it to be the knock of opportunity. Jack didn't even have to spin around to know who it was. It was Corman Todd. He owned a food truck in the park as well. His truck was called soles and shoestrings. They sold whatever the catch of the day was with fries, and he ended the day with a nice story to entertain those who wanted to get the leftovers of the day for free. The quantity would vary, but the quality wouldn't, and everyone wanted to get a taste at the end of the day.

Jack turned to face Corman. Corman looked at the contraption and ran his hand over his beard.

"I'm never sure if you're going to be in a different part of the park or if you are just late working on your items."

Jack wished Corman would assume he was at the park. That way, he would have more peace of mind and not have to be bothered by the questions that he always had to face when Corman arrived.

"I'm almost ready to leave."

Corman looked at the machine and then nodded. "So, is this the famous dog feeder?"

"I don't know that it's famous, but you are correct when you call it the dog feeder."

"It came out well."

Jack nodded and then turned to clean his hands. Corman didn't seem to understand why Jack built items. But he was a supportive friend who said all of his inventions came out well.

"Thanks."

Jack began to clean his tools and put them in their proper places on the shelves.

"I'm thinking we should be a little closer to each other. The competition is starting to pick up with kiosks that sell trinkets getting permits in the park."

Jack had heard the beginnings of this argument for the last couple of months. It was his signal that the sales at Corman's truck were flagging.

"It's not about competition, Corman. I think you need to think about having a changing menu. It's hard to supply the same thing all the time and expect it to be brand new to people.

Corman sighed. "I've heard you say that before. Maybe we should take a look at my offerings."

Jack put his equipment up and tried not to let his shoulders tense up from the words. The words weren't new, and Jack knew they weren't genuine either.

"Great. That will give us some time to meet for dinner sometime."

Jack listened to Corman go on about the good old days when the other rolling kiosks weren't there. He talks about how Jack's ideas had more "legs" than anything that he'd come up with, and again, Jack tried his best not to criticize openly. Jack had been down this road before, and he didn't want to remind Corman that he wasn't going to offer any new ideas at their dinner. In fact, If Corman ever took notes on what he actually said, he would have all the information that he needed.

"Hey, Jack. I want you to know that I'm grateful that you're around. You're a little more relaxed than I am when it comes to business, but you have solid ideas that I wouldn't think about." Jack nodded and braced himself for the inevitable back slap that would cause him to cough if he wasn't prepared. Jack didn't want to remind him that all of the ideas that he suggested to him he also used on his truck, and they had helped him to fight that "competition" he perceived.

Jack was happy that he had an occupation that paid homage to his family and was consistent. He knew running a truck wasn't his life goal, but it was enough for now, he supposed. His sister Gloria thought it was a steady gig. He had started it when he arrived at Inheritance Bay to be able to put food on the table.

As Corman left and Jack finished up with his tools, he looked at his workshop and a sense of pride and accomplishment came over him. Jack knew that he had to leave the love of his life, which was making things, to go back to his day job that required him to think about the price of lobster and other sea living creatures that might make the menu this week.

A sharp rap sounded on his garage door. Jack shook his head and wondered what Corman could have forgotten. Then the rap happened again. When Jack opened the door to the garage, he expected to see his friend, who was six foot and had brown hair, but instead, he saw a five-foot-three-inch woman with sable brown hair. She was dressed in blue jeans and an oversized lumberjack shirt. The woman had an oval face, and from her pinched expression, she was not happy. What caught his attention the most was her eyes, which were glorious in her fury.

"Hello, Jack!" she sneered.

Jack looked at Kathy and wondered what had brought her here. She was by far the most intriguing woman he had ever met. Her temperament seemed to be as mercurial as the weather, but no matter her mood, Jack was fascinated by the woman.

"Hello, Kathy. I didn't realize we had an appointment today."

He watched her pull herself to her full five-foot-three and then walk into his garage. He stepped back to give her room, but he could see the light of victory in her gaze.

"We didn't have an appointment, but I'm here on business."

"On business? You might have mixed up a meeting, maybe?" Jack said as he looked at a fidgeting Kathy in front of him.

Kathy crossed her arms in front of her chest, and Jack thought she looked cute but didn't dare to smile.

"You can stop smirking as if your looks have any effect on me. I didn't mix up any meetings at all. I'm here to see you, Mr. Jack Danvers."

Jack couldn't wait to see what she wanted. He had admired Kathy from afar, and now seeing her upfront, he could confirm that she was as dynamic as she appeared.

"Did you come down to Inheritance Bay just to see me?"

"I came down to set you straight, not to make a nice-nice social call."

"To set me straight? What was it that I've done that you felt as though you needed to come and set me straight?"

"Well, it seems as though you have been a very busy person," Kathy said with a raised eyebrow.

"What is it that I've done that was so offensive?" Jack tried to think over the times he had met Kathy, and nothing came to mind.

"You are a homewrecker!" Jack was expecting a lot of things, but that surely wasn't one of them. It was kind of comical if you really thought about it. Gloria, his sister, had been badgering him to get out more and find a woman. She was sure that the right one was out there for him.

"I'm pretty sure I'm going to need some more clues to understand how you think I am a homewrecker, and whose home am I wrecking?"

"Gloria, your sister."

"My sister is all the family I have left, and I would never do anything to hurt her or Reid as they start their lives together."

"Well, it seems you are quick to remind a person that Gloria is your family."

Jack wasn't sure where this was going, but he was sure the fireball was mistaken, whatever it was that put her on the path.

"I'm rather proud that Gloria is related to me. It shows there might be some chance of me finding some good in me."

He could see that his statement had taken a bit of the wind out of her sails. She frowned and then started to tap her foot in front of him.

"Well, Mr. 'All In For The Family,' we are big on the family too, but we know how to make sure we don't leave anyone out. Reid knows that you've been there for Gloria and that you always will be there. However, you not inviting Reid when you are grieving or remembering your past keeps him on the outside and stops Gloria and Reid from sharing all things."

Jack listened to Kathy, and at first, the words that came to mind was that she was overreacting, but then he remembered when they met for their father's yearly remembrance. She had been there, but she had been distracted. He thought she was just remembering the past, but now he could see that maybe he had been obtuse to her feelings. He must have taken too long to respond, and that gave Kathy the space to jump in.

"I'm surprised you'd do that kind of thing, considering how much you say you care about her."

"How much I say I care about her?" Jack echoed. He could see that Kathy was passionate, but the accusation stung. The attack put him on the defensive because he wasn't sure he was right.

"I'm not saying you don't care. What I mean is you don't seem to be ready to share your sister with her future husband. You are her brother, but she needs to have a life separate from you and depend on him."

Jack stepped back and took the time to close the garage door and think about what was being said.

"Kathy, forgive me for being indelicate, but how did you become separated from your parents?"

Kathy's eyes narrowed, and she looked at him for a moment before answering. "She left."

Jack nodded. "I understand that when a parent leaves a child, there are scars that may never heal. However, when a parent dies and leaves a family with nobody to mourn over and no closure of what their last minutes were like, it's an open wound that can never heal. Pain is pain, so I don't want you to think I'm comparing that at all.

"Gloria and I had questions about what happened and what could have been. We had a mother who didn't know how to process the event and just refused to talk of his passing as a death. Instead of processing that loss with us, we were taught he left us for another woman. It wasn't until later that we understood that the woman was the sea. We share a lot in common, Kathy. We don't think about it anymore, but I'm Gloria's stepbrother. The loss of our father wasn't just the loss of a parent. It was also a connection between us."

Kathy focused on him intently, like she was taking in his every word. He hoped that he hadn't offended her, but he wanted her to understand how they had gotten here.

"I hear you, Jack, but the issue remains the same. People grow up, and we have issues. We have problems that we have to deal with, but life goes on. It's not fair or just sometimes. Sometimes it just is. What I do know is that if you care for someone, then you want them to be happy. Even if that means you need to take your total overprotective, caveman alpha male self out of the way."

Jack gave her a smile and leaned against the door.

"Alpha male? Is that how you see me? Because I'm completely on board with that."

Kathy opened her mouth, and nothing came out. Then she closed her eyes and took a deep breath, and let it out.

"Take your club and knock some sense into yourself. Don't be the obstacle here."

Jack's smile faded from his mouth, and he allowed Kath's words to sink into his head. His sister didn't need just him anymore, but he had to admit he was the one holding on here. He had been so protective of Gloria when she arrived, and now she had come out of her shell and was with a man that Jack had to admit he admired grudgingly.

"Okay, you're right. I'll work on it."

Kathy looked over her shoulder and then leaned to the side and looked around him. Jack looked behind him too, thinking she had seen something but, what, he couldn't imagine. Kathy didn't seem the squeamish kind when it came to bugs.

She shrugged. "What happened? Did you switch with a clone?"

"What are you talking about?" Jack said, confused.

"I mean, you just agree, like that?"

Jack smiled.

"Listen, this is my thought on business and life. If you find out that you are wrong, don't fight it. Accept what is and make the best of the situation."

"Make the best of it?" Kathy echoed with a raised eyebrow and a look of disbelief on her face.

"Yes, and in that vein, I would like to ask you out."

"Ask me out?"

"Yes, you know it's an old caveman ritual. A man goes to a woman and gives a tug on her hair. She then turns and gives him a nod, and he hunts food for them, and they eat outside under the stars."

Kathy stopped and then burst forth laughing.

"First of all, the last boy who tugged my hair was Timothy Peterson, and when he did, Reid had a talk with him about it. Second, you hunting our food, while interesting, isn't tempting enough when I think about the outdoor bugs." Kathy shook her head and walked around Jack.

"So that's it? You're not going to answer me?" he said with his best smile and puppy dog eyes.

Kathy looked at him incredulously. "Listen up,

Mr. I'm So Charming All Will Fall. I'm not interested in going on a date with you. I came to do some business, and you were a side note. So, if you will excuse me."

Jack stepped aside, and she left. He wasn't sure what it was about her, but that was the longest conversation he had engaged in with a woman who wasn't Gloria in months. There was something special about Kathy that he wanted to follow up on. Now all he had to do was to get her to agree.

CHAPTER 3

*O*kay, there might be a reason she had seen and heard that women sigh over Jack Danvers. If Kathy were honest, she'd confess to hearing the rumors about the hot guy who sells lobster in the park. She hadn't come to meet the most eligible man in the park. She had come to set a stubborn man in his place and to make him aware of the error of his ways. She'd been prepared to step in and lay down some justice. Instead, he had accepted her words and then asked her out to dinner. What was that even about?

More importantly, Kathy couldn't figure out what was going on when she looked back on how easily he had accepted her answer or how reasonable he had been. When she thought about how she had been so gung-ho to come out and set him right, she could see that Jack was an oddity, and she had called him a caveman. After calling him a caveman, he had asked her out. He couldn't have been serious.

Kathy hadn't been dating because she didn't

believe anyone saw her these days. Oh, if she were honest, she would have to say the other reason she hadn't been dating was that she didn't trust. Besides, she had seen the effects of love. It was always temporary and hurtful. Now that Reid had found love, he, of course, thought she needed to get out more. While she may have agreed that she could get out some more, what she was sure of was that a man didn't go out with you after you called him an evolutionary throwback.

Kathy wanted to say that Jack didn't understand what she had been saying. Maybe the reason he had decided to ask her out on a date had more to do with the idea of covering up that he wasn't as insensitive as she had originally thought. Kathy shook her head and wondered why she was even thinking about this. Jack couldn't really be interested in her after all. No one was really interested in her, and she made sure to go out of her way that no one noticed her. Besides, Kathy had a plan, and she needed to stick to it. The first part of the plan was to make sure that Reid would be happy. Now that she had made sure that Jack wouldn't interfere with Reid's life, she could go on with her part of the plan.

While Kathy had been muttering and going over the meeting between her and Jack, she had walked two blocks to her waiting car. After she sidled into the leather car, the window came down, and the driver asked in a low voice.

"Miss, where are we going?"

That was the question of the hour. Where was she going? She hated to admit it to herself, but what she really wanted to do was to go back into that garage and say yes to Jack. She didn't really understand why she wanted to say yes to Jack. I mean, it wasn't like no one else had asked her out. Kathy thought that it was his ability to be so open to change that made him seem more trustworthy. It was madness to decide to go out on a date with Jack.

Kathy looked up to see the chauffeurs, eyes looking back at her in the rearview mirror. She waved her hand so that the driver would know she was still deciding. Kathy let her head fall back against the headrest in the back seat. What was the problem? Why was she having such a huge issue about just telling the driver to take her back home? Kathy nibbled her bottom lip and tried to work her way through this latest dilemma. She knew that she was becoming more emotional because it was getting time to leave.

If she was going to leave and be on her own, the least she could do was experience as much as possible before she left. How many other Jack Danvers would show up to ask her out on a date? What does she really know about Jack, anyway? This would be one of those times that Kathy really regretted that she wasn't able to make more female friends. She had seen how those other women did it in the movies all the time. She couldn't call anyone, though, because she would have to explain why she had come down here, to begin with. On top of it all, she had already told Jack that she had other plans, and that was why she couldn't go out on the date with him. Kathy kept her eyes closed and tried to think through this latest problem.

Kathy started to put a plan together, and she was sure she could do it if she acted quickly.

She tapped on the diving screen and called out, "Drive around the bay."

The next thing Kathy did was call Jack.

"Hello?"

"I've had an opening in my schedule. Where did you want to do this meeting?"

"You mean the date?"

Kathy shook her head and sighed. "Yes, that's what I said," she muttered.

"I am still where you left me. Are you close?"

"No, I'm on the move."

"You're on the moving talking to me as you're driving?" Jack asked.

Kathy grunted. "Before you ask, no, I am not driving and talking on the phone at the same time. I am in the car with the driver."

"Ah, yes, I forgot you do make some extra coin on the side."

Kathy almost laughed. She didn't consider being on the Forbes list, even if it was at the bottom as making extra coin, but it sounded cute when he said it.

"If the rumors are to be believed, yes, I do make an extra coin or two on the side," Kathy said with a smile on her face.

"Does the lady have any preference on where she would like to eat dinner?"

"I hear there's this nice swanky place in the park that sells lobster."

Jack snorted.

"I hope you don't think that just because I don't make a side coin that you're going to go on a cheap date."

"I wasn't thinking that it was going to be a cheap date. I was just trying to make it convenient for you."

"I knew there was a reason I liked you, Kathy. While I appreciate your concern, I wouldn't have made the offer if I wasn't able to provide the quality experience that you deserve."

Kathy was speechless. A quality experience that she deserved? She almost giggled at the thought.

"I like sashimi."

"I like Sushi," he replied.

Kathy's grin grew. "No, I didn't say sushi. I like Sashimi. You know, the raw fish, no rice."

There was no sound on the phone, and for a moment, Kathy thought she had reached his limit.

"Are you there?" she asked tentatively.

"Yes, I found the place. If the lady would like sashimi, so be it."

Curiosity wouldn't let her let it alone. "I noticed the pause. Is there an issue?"

"No, I just want to find a place we can eat without all of Inheritance Bay watching. You know how it is in a small town. As soon as you arrived, I'm sure it was news, and going to the sushi house on the bay is inviting rumors. I wouldn't want to infringe on your privacy because I know you guard it."

Kathy wondered how many people actually noticed that she guarded her privacy. There was something in the fact that he had been looking at her likes and her wants that made her pause.

"Thank you."

"I haven't even begun to try to impress you, but if that works, then there's hope I'll be a superstar. Do you want to meet me at the restaurant, or do you want me to come and pick you up?"

"Send me the address, and I'll meet you there."

"Smart girl. You're not quite sure whether or not I'm going to be that crazy person or not. Better to meet in public. I knew there were all sorts of reasons that I liked you, Kathy."

Kathy couldn't stop the small giggle that escaped.

"I'll send the address in ten minutes."

"You know my number."

"My caller id does," he said. She wanted to say duh out loud. She wasn't even out on a date with this man, and she was acting weird. She needed to get to the other part of her plan.

"Well, I have some things to take care of, so I'll see you later."

"I look forward to it, Kathy."

Kathy hung up the phone and rested her head against the car. She didn't know why Jack affected her so, but she was determined to get this out of her system and move on. If she said it enough times, she'd believe it too. Picking up her phone, she made two calls. The first call was to leave a message with Reid that she was visiting and taking off business. The next call would help her cover up this madness.

~

Traci looked at the phone ringing and couldn't believe her bad luck. If she had been able to leave ten minutes earlier, this wouldn't have even had been an issue. Resignedly, she clicked on the phone, and Kathy's face came into view. Traci tried to angle herself, so her back was against the wall.

"Hey, Kathy," Traci said, trying to add some sort of lightness to her voice.

"Traci, thank goodness I caught you. I know this is going to sound so crazy, but I need a favor."

Traci looked at Kathy, and she seemed okay. From the video, it looked like Kathy was in the car. The only problem that Traci could see was that Kathy looked a bit nervous.

"You know you have me on pins and needles because you never ask for a favor."

"I know, I know. But this time, I've managed to do something that I need some help to get out of, and I wanted to know if you could do me a favor."

"First—you're safe, right?"

Kathy tucked a strand of hair behind her ear and nodded.

"I'm not in any physical danger. I've just been stupid."

The tension left Traci's body; Traci leaned back and smiled.

"This kind of lapse in judgment only seems to come about when dealing with the opposite sex. Tell me, Kathy is this about a man?"

Tracy watched the telltale blush creep up Kathy's cheeks.

"Go for it. I won't rag you now, but you've got to tell me later, okay?"

Kathy nodded.

"If anyone asks, I came to Inheritance Bay to see you."

Traci nodded and waved her off. She saw Kathy fidgeting with her phone and smiled. This wasn't going to be the moment when she gets caught at all.

"Of course, you came to see me. No problem.

Oh, and when you did this, did we go somewhere in particular?" Traci said, smiling at how people changed when they were in relationships or trying to figure them out.

"I think sticking with the truth as much as possible is best. I'm looking up your location now and we can go from—"

"What? Kathy, stop!"

Traci's words were too late. When Kathy looked at her in the video, it was confirmed on her face that the uncomfortable situation that she was trying to avoid had just become a reality.

"Traci?"

Traci leaned back against the wall and waited for the question to come. Before Kathy could ask anything, a woman opened the door to the room Traci was in.

"Mrs. Chance, here are your results. Let us know if we can be of any more assistance to you," the young lady dressed in nurse's white said in a low, calming voice.

"Thank you for everything," Traci replied to the retreating figure of the nurse.

"Traci?"

Realizing that not looking directly into the video wasn't going to make this problem go away, Traci looked at Kathy.

"Traci, your phone says you're at a Fertility Clinic."

The statement hung in the air between them. Traci nodded and then looked Kathy directly in the eye.

"Well, it seems like you're not the only one who is going to need a favor," Traci said. She hadn't wanted anyone to know until she had talked to her husband Vincent. Traci, more than most, should have known how the best-laid plans go south quickly. She could manage this, she just needed to talk to her orphan husband, who was sure that he would make an awful dad, and that she wanted to have a baby. Traci slumped in the chair. She had a feeling that this was just the beginning of how south this plan was about to go.

CHAPTER 4

*K*athy was grateful for the chauffeur. She needed the dinner to not distract her from thinking about Traci, where she was, and what it could mean. Instead, the driver brought her to Umi's, the premier restaurant on the outskirts of Inheritance Bay. Kathy wanted to make sure that the table wasn't in the middle of the room. She completely understood what Jack was saying about being in Inheritance Bay and everyone knowing their business if they were seen together.

However, Kathy had been trained by overzealous reporters and knew that no matter where she went, as long as she had money, there would always be someone trying to spy on her. With her natural predilection to privacy, she always liked to be on the side, facing the door, and preferably in a corner.

Kathy looked around the upscale restaurant, and the old feelings of being watched encroached upon her. It was almost like a specter of gloom followed her, weighing her down with anxiety and apprehension.

It was one of the reasons that she was seeing a therapist to manage her anxiety. Not even the chipper voice of the hostess could stop her spiral of stress.

"Can I help you?" the hostess asked.

Kathy gave a jerky nod.

"I have a reservation here with Jack Da—"

The hostess cut her off. "Of course, Mr. Danvers. Come this way."

Kathy wasn't sure how to feel about the fact that the hostess knew who Jack was. As she followed the young lady, Kathy's trepidation grew as she was led to a table in the middle of the floor.

"Ah, is there another table on the side, perhaps?"

The hostess looked confused, and then as if she couldn't be bothered trying to figure out people, the hostess plastered another smile on her face and then took her to a side table that was just what Kathy was looking for.

Just as Kathy was settling down at the table, Jack came into the restaurant. Kathy watched him scan the restaurant and then focus on her and make a beeline for her. His smile was bright, and his step eager. Kathy had to wonder, was all of that because he was happy to meet her?

When he got to the table, he looked over his shoulder and then at their location and how it was fairly dark and removed from the rest of the diners. Kathy waited for him to ask to be moved, but instead, he took a seat and then leaned toward her.

"I can see that meeting outside of Inheritance Bay wasn't enough. If I had known you were so ashamed of being seen with me, I might have suggested that we just eat in," Jack said with a smile.

Kathy looked at him, and she can't believe he is joking about where they are sitting. She was so used to everyone being careful around her regarding her condition that it had become a shield of sorts.

When he put his napkin on his lap and looked up, he smirked.

"So, was I supposed to wait until the third or fourth date before I joked around?"

And just like that, with just a few words, Jack managed to get through Kathy's defenses. Everyone else had treated her as if she were going to break at any moment, but not Jack. He seemed to have an innate understanding about what she could and could not do. Ultimately, it was the idea that he treated her just as if she were everyone else. She knew that he had heard the stories about how she rarely came out of the house. It was no secret that she had some sort of anxiety disorder that gave her pause about being in public.

Yet with one sentence, he had managed to get through a barrier that many others had died at the gate of.

Kathy could feel the smile break out across her face.

"I'm going to order the most expensive things on the menu for that," she teased.

Jack leaned across the table. "Well, then, I guess it's a good thing I brought my hand moisturizer to help if I have to wash dishes."

Kathy's hands went over her mouth, and she had to hold the laughter inside.

"Come on; we're outside of town. Go ahead and

make some noise. It will do wonders for my reputation that I've managed to make you laugh."

Kathy shook her head and picked up the menu, trying to distract him.

"What are you going to eat?" she asked.

"I don't know what I'm going to eat yet. I have to see how expensive your meal is going to be. Maybe you'll switch roles tonight, and I'll be the one to order a small side salad with an appetizer. You know, I want you to understand that I am concerned about my figure, and I only want to look my best when I'm with you."

Kathy was intrigued by his obvious teasing and flirting. No man had felt like they could approach her, but Jack was no ordinary man.

"How was your business meeting?"

"It definitely wasn't what I was expecting. It ran shorter than I thought it needed to, and the findings are still unclear," Kathy said, thinking about Traci and what it meant where she was.

"That doesn't sound like you. I would have thought that you would have come completely prepared for the meeting."

Kathy nodded and had to remember to keep her head in the game. Kathy couldn't reconcile why, but she didn't want there to be a lie between them.

"The truth of the matter is, the meeting was very last minute. I actually arranged the meeting because I was already here," Kathy confessed.

Jack smiled and raised an eyebrow. "Am I hearing this correctly? Are you saying that you came out just to see me?" Jack said, holding his hand to his chest in mock surprise.

Kathy grinned. "Are you forgetting what happened when I got here?"

"Ah, yes. We had a heated conversation about the roles of family and loved ones. Which in case I didn't say before or I wasn't clear, you were totally right to call me out on. In fact, if you want to have any type of conversation with me and call me out, so we have to go to dinner, I'm open for criticism."

"Really?" Kathy asked. Jack was turning out to be a completely different man than Kathy had painted him to be.

Jack held up his hand and started to count off three fingers.

"These are the three things that I've learned from my sister which has helped me survive women. One, it's okay to be wrong even if I'm right. Me telling my sister she was wrong was never as effective as us talking it out, and her coming to the conclusion that she might be wrong. Two, when you don't know something, just confess you are lost. Trying to guess what is going on has never worked, and if anything, it opens up a can of worms of other things that would never have been mentioned. Three, find a safe space to talk. Sometimes it's in a mall, and sometimes it's over dinner. Wherever the safe place is, make sure you keep it pure by not arguing there and never leaving the place with her being bitter."

Kathy nodded. "Good rules." Kathy didn't want to say those were the wisest, most common-sense rules she had heard in a while. She didn't have to comment on them because the waiter came and took their order. After the waiter had left, she looked around the restaurant and remembered how the hostess had known him right away.

"So, everyone sees you in the park. When do you have the time to find a place outside of the bay?" Kathy asked. "I mean, according to the local gossip, not that I listen to that, but if I did, all I'm saying is that they all say you spend all of your time in the food truck in the park."

"Well, I'm glad that you don't listen to that kind of gossip. But to be fair to all of them, it is true that I spend a lot of time in the park. However, I also need to do a lot of research in other parks and places, and so I find myself often trekking out to festivals and small events where people come to showcase their specialty wares."

It was at his mention that he needed to travel and be around groups of people in order to learn new things that Kathy could feel herself starting to retract.

"Is there something wrong?" Jack asked.

Kathy didn't want to squirm in her seat, but she wasn't sure she could stop herself. This was one of the problems of being with someone who was so attentive to all of her moods. In the beginning, it was the greatest thing to have a man infatuated with you enough in order to be able to know what you were feeling before you spoke. However, it was times like this when her privacy was more important than the communion between two people.

"There's nothing wrong. I'm just listening." It wasn't the most convincing statement Kathy had ever made, but it would do in a pinch. This was a problem. Jack was so social. Not that Kathy was thinking of doing anything with him long-term or anything, but if she were, this social thing wasn't for her.

"I hear that the bay has a whole celebration every year as well as sponsors festivals. Since you have some well-known potters here and the value of the homes are going up as well, the bay festivals will rival their next-door neighbors."

"It's true there has been a concentrated effort to bring more people into this very peaceful town." What else could Kathy say at this moment? She couldn't explain to him that one of the things that were going wrong at Inheritance Bay was that more people were coming. It was going to take away one more place that she could potentially go and not have to worry about too many people being there. There it was again, coming up in the middle of her life. All right, her inability to be around large groups of people was definitely a drawback.

"So, what is the real reason that we're eating in the place outside of the bay? Is it because you do secret clandestine work?"

Kathy didn't even know where to begin. The only thing she could keep thinking about was that he wanted to be around large groups of people in order to learn new things, and that was the last thing she ever wanted to do.

"One of the many reasons that I wanted to eat outside of the Bay is because you are right. A lot of people know that I am the one who suggests new projects and researches projects that might make money. I seem to have a very good success rate and intuition about these things, and it leads people to come looking for me, especially in a town that's growing." Kathy took a sip of water and kept on talking. "Reid really wanted to concentrate on his ranch, and with my finding new businesses it keeps things calm between Reid and Mr. Dane, our lawyer."

"Gloria has said that he's mercurial."

Kathy wanted to laugh out loud. Of course, Gloria would come up with some diplomatic way to describe Mr. Dane.

"Mercurial, that is definitely a new word that I have heard applied to Mr. Dane. When everyone first meets Mr. Dane, they all think he is the kindest man you will ever meet. It takes time for Mr. Dane to get a clear picture of what he thinks he needs from you and what you should be doing. When Patty was alive, she was essentially his Pitbull."

"Her Pitbull? Well, I have to say I've only had one or two dealings with Mr. Dane. He helped me out when I was getting some permits and setting up my truck. I found him to be very precise, if anything. However, I have to say I am constantly intrigued by everybody else's viewpoint of this man."

Kathy cocked her head to the side and looked at Jack. "Tell me a joke. Do you like puzzles?"

"I have to admit that I do."

Kathy wasn't surprised by that answer. She really just wanted him to confirm it.

"Well, if you're really into puzzles, then you will probably get along with Mr. Dane famously. There are all sorts of rumors surrounding him and Patty. As a result, it always seemed as though Mr. Dane was the stand-in father figure for everybody. Whenever Patty needed to have one of those conversations with the boys, she always called him. Patty trusted Mr. Dane so much that she let him check up on everyone. In the beginning, it probably wasn't so bad. then as everyone started to figure out what they wanted to do, and maybe it wasn't always to make money and go into companies, he would have something to say."

"Why does it matter what he has to say?"

Kathy sighed. "Well, the crux of the matter is, this time, the boys went out and made money, and they always gave a percentage to Patty. It was their way of making sure that she never wanted for any money, just in case. She didn't have to say what she did with her part of the percentage. She didn't have to explain to anyone what had happened, but everyone gave it to her. What they didn't realize was she was, in turn, letting Mr. Dane manage it. Not to say that Mr. Dane is a bad person. He's not. He's just not very flexible for people who decide they want to go do something else, and there is no obvious money path."

Jack nodded in understanding. "So, you think that now Patti has passed on, he's doing it for his own profit?"

Kathy shook her head. "If you want to know the truth, I really think he's doing this in memory of Patty. I think that he is helping everyone stay on the right track to being successful. The problem is that Reid doesn't want to do that anymore. So, in order to keep him appeased, I have been filling in, and so far, it seems like it's working."

"So, you do all of it by yourself?" Jack asked.

"No, I don't. It's a partnership. I may find the idea and look at it and think that it's okay, but Reid has that practical experience of knowing what's trending."

Jack looked confused. "So, Mr. Dane doesn't know that the both of you contribute?"

"He's not the boogie man. He's just set in his ways. He wants us all to be stable and happy. He also thinks that money can come and go quickly if you don't make more of it and watch it. "

"So, it's safe to say you're used to dating men who show up in Forbes magazine?" Jack asked.

Kathy thought about the question, and for a moment, she had to think about it. It was true she rarely, if ever, dated, and if she did, it was someone on the cover of a money magazine. They usually invited her to dine in a private place that was bought out just for them.

"I can tell from your silence that I've hit it on the head. Well, I shall not let my average joe compadres down. I will be paying for this meal, and if tasked to do so, I will face the all-knowing Mr. Dane for you," Jack proclaimed.

Kathy laughed. "While Reid builds his therapy ranch, Mr. Dane can get a bit nosy, but I can handle him. Thank you, though, for offering."

"So, the town rumor says you are a self-imposed hermit most of the time. Will you tell me why?" Jack asked.

"Wow. You just jump right in it, don't you?" Kathy said, letting small breaths out of her mouth and trying to get a grip on her heartbeat.

"You can always say it's none of my business."

For a minute, Kathy considered it.

CHAPTER 5

*J*ack knew Kathy was thinking about whether she wanted to answer the question. There was something about Kathy that made him want to know everything about her. He was about to change the subject when she took a breath and started to speak.

"I had a hard time of it before Reid. I know people look at me now and think I'm eccentric or just stuck up because I won't go certain places and be around too many people, but when you are young in a foster care system that doesn't have enough people to check on every child, you learn how to be quiet and disappear in the background. Reid gives me my space when I need to be alone while still being around."

Jack could hear all of the words and feelings she wasn't saying. He understood that there were stories and hurts from behind her, words that she couldn't reveal to other people. There was a small part of him that was angry. He was angry that she even had to go through any of those things. But he also realized that it was her going through those things that made her the amazing woman she was today.

"Gloria says that Reid is beating himself up for not finding you sooner," Jack confessed.

"Reid takes too much onto himself. The truth of the matter is, before Reid had found me, I had already decided to stop."

"Stop what?"

"I had decided to stop trying to do anything in life. I had decided to stop participating or being around people because I just couldn't trust them. I was just going to hermit up in my room and just let things go as they could. Before we came, I was just tired and exhausted with life. You don't look so surprised."

"Life has a way of humbling us all in its own time. I'm just a little surprised that the world allowed you to keep to yourself since you are so talented. Tell me, what do you think about food trucks? Good or bad long-term investment?" Jack asked Kathy.

Kathy laughed. "I'm not going to fall into that trap."

"Trap?" Jack echoed.

Kathy nodded as the food came, and they began to eat.

"Do you know how many people ask me if their businesses will make it or what they should do to save it? It doesn't work that way. I'm not a fortune teller."

Jack sat back and held his hand to his chest. "What?! Are you sure?"

Kathy laughed and nodded. "I'm sorry to disappoint you, but I'm just me."

Jack shook his head. "You are many things but never a disappointment."

Kathy looked at him for a moment and then continued to eat. Then she broke the silence. "I'm surprised how good the food was."

Jack smiled. "I can see you enjoyed it. I mean, I barely got a bite," he said.

"Barely got a bite? Are you kidding? I saw you inhale that plate by you, and I have no idea what was on that plate," she said with laughter in her voice.

Jack looked at the plate. He was thoroughly enjoying Kathy like this. She was carefree and relaxed. He could see that she had gone through struggles, but it hadn't taken away the inner joy of living. He admired her and knew for sure that he wanted to see her again. Now the only thing he needed to do was to convince her that it was a good idea. They both heard Cathy's phone go off. It was a small beep, but it was enough for her to take a look. Jack didn't say anything. He just waited. He could tell from the way that Kathy's lips pursed that whoever it was, she was not exactly thrilled.

"Is everything okay?"

Kathy looked up at him, frustrated. "Everything is fine. It's just Reid being Reid."

"What does that even mean?"

"What it means is that my brother is waiting for me to return back home as soon as this dinner is over."

"You're going to leave me right after dinner? I was sure that this wouldn't be a problem. Both of us brought out our IDs. He must know that you're over the age of eighteen."

Jack watched Cathy smile and then put her phone back into her bag.

"My brother is very aware of how old I am, and he is also very concerned about my welfare."

"Did you, by chance, tell him that you were having dinner with me?" Jack asked, not wanting to look at her.

"I did mention that I was with you, but—"

Jack started laughing.

"Okay, obviously, this is some man thing, and you're going to bring me up to speed any moment now," Kathy said, looking less than pleased at Jack. Jack held up his hands in defense.

"Forgive me. I don't mean to make it seem like I was trying to mansplain anything. I just can't imagine what your brother's face would look like when you told him you were going on a date with me."

"A date? I didn't tell him it was a date. Just dinner."

Jack sat back and smiled at Kathy.

"Well, let me be the one to say it in case there was any doubt. This is our first date. In fact, we are running ahead of schedule," Jack said wryly.

"Ahead of schedule?"

"Yes, we are on our first date. We've already had our first fight, and we are hiding from the public so no one will know about us. I would have to say we are ahead of schedule in a nice way."

Kathy looked at him, shocked. "You are crazy."

"I think you might be right. It seems I'm way taken with you, as the old wordsmiths would say."

"Really?" she asked incredulously.

"Ah, I see the lady needs some convincing."

"First, you didn't come to find me. I came to put you in your place, remember?"

"Yes, but then when your brilliance once again showed upon me, it was clear," Jack said with a smile.

"Okay, what were you before you opened the Claw House, some marketing person?" she teased.

Jack sobered as memories flooded him of what was.

"I wasn't some kind of marketing person. I have always been handy and loved to cook. I tried to use those skills whenever I could because they brought me the greatest joy. I was hoping that you would come with me because today is one of those days where I indulge in my joy."

"Exactly what are you going to be doing?" Kathy asked. Jack could see that her curiosity was peaked.

"Now, where is the excitement if I tell you exactly what it is?"

Jack could see that she was considering whether she wanted to go.

"So, you want me to make a decision to go somewhere with you, and you're not going to tell me where it is? Whatever this place or thing is would have to be good enough to listen to my brother go on and on about my safety and how he only wants what is best for me."

"If you'd like, I can call him and let him know you are in good hands with me, "Jack volunteered.

Kathy snorted and then composed herself. "Let me give you a bit of advice, Jack. Never call someone's brother and say she's in good hands with you, and she won't be coming home on time either."

Jack stopped and then laughed with her. "Okay,

you're right I can't see that going well if Gloria said that either."

"So, spill it!"

"Well, once upon a time, I was paralyzed, and I couldn't do things for myself. So, I'm oh, so aware of how people always staring, feeling bad for something they couldn't fix, can be a pain."

~

Reid stood looking out of the window. There was no reason for him to be nervous. Kathy was a grown woman and didn't need a keeper.

"You know, she won't appreciate you standing at the door waiting for her, right?" He turned to look at his wife, Gloria, sitting on the sofa, looking casual and unconcerned. Gloria had already left her mark on the room. Once upon a time, the house had been decorated with stoic, dark furniture. Now, everywhere you went, there was a hint of a flower of some kind. The tables all had an inlay of pearl roses on the perimeter. The carpet now had a light hint of a floral print on the perimeter. The valances had small periwinkle blue flowers on them. Nothing had escaped Gloria. When Reid asked why she said that flowers represented hope to her. He wasn't sure if that was true, but he would do anything to make Gloria happy.

After their wedding at Thanksgiving, he had hoped he would be past the jealousies of a new relationship. Instead, Reid found himself still at the mercy of jealousies he thought were long gone.

It seemed as though she was not going to be the

only woman who was on his mind tonight. Kathy had called and said that she was in town, and Reid expected her to be back any moment. After all, she was out with Jack, Gloria's brother. The two of them were an odd pair. It was as if sometimes they got along, and then sometimes they didn't. Reid didn't really care either which way. His only concern was for Kathy. He had been looking for her at an early age when they were separated as children. It had taken him far longer to find her than he'd thought. In the interim, she had been through a lot of rough houses, and it showed by her need to be alone and not wanting to go out into public. Every time Kathy shied away from going out into public, it was like a knife in Reid's heart. It was just another reminder that he had failed her and had not found her soon enough.

"Stop beating yourself up over there," Gloria said from the couch.

"I'm not beating myself up. I'm just being concerned," Reid said as he walked over to sit on the couch beside Gloria.

"I'm glad that we actually have this time, Reid because I wanted to talk to you."

"I don't remember any good conversation starting with a woman who says, 'I want to talk to you,'" Reid said sarcastically.

"Well, then, I guess we are about to break the mold," Gloria said as she scooted over to make room for Reid.

Reid gave her another look and then nodded. Gloria laughed and then pushed him on the shoulder.

Reid opened one eye at a time and waited for

Gloria to speak. She took his hands into hers and then brought them to her lips to kiss.

"Wow, this is going to be a big one, huh?" Reid whispered.

"I hope not. I've been watching you work with the kids and the horses, and I want you to know that I feel really inspired, and I am so proud of what you're doing on the ranch."

He had to admit this wasn't where he thought the conversation was going to go.

"Thank you. You know, it's been a life dream of mine to have a therapeutic ranch, and with Kathy's help, I've really been able to get it up and going."

"I wanted to run an idea by you first."

"Okay."

"I have been volunteering with the speech therapist, and I think I want to do that as well."

Reid looked at Gloria, and he was happy and frustrated at the same time.

"Gloria, that's a big step. You know I believe in you, and I think that you can do anything, but I also want to make sure you don't take on too much, either."

Gloria sat back on the couch, and she tossed her sable brown hair over her shoulder.

"Okay, Reid. What's wrong?"

"Nothing is wrong. I just thought you really enjoyed organizing things, and this is a big jump. The kids that come here are hurting and already need so much. I wasn't sure if you were prepared for that kind of commitment to children. "

The minute the words had left Reid's mouth, he wished he could bring them back.

"You think I can't work with children?" Gloria whispered in the room.

"No, that's not it at all. I think that you are amazing at your job, and I was just thinking about what a huge change it would be for you."

Gloria stood up from the couch and then looked at Reid.

"You know, I thought you would be happy that I wanted to do something with you. I thought you would think this was a great idea for me to work side by side with you, and instead, I get the feeling that you either think I can't do it or that I shouldn't be around kids. I'm not sure which one it is, but neither one makes me feel like you think a whole lot of me."

Reid stood up and pulled Gloria into his arms. She went reluctantly and was a bit stiff. He stepped away from her and then tucked a hair behind her ear.

"Please, Gloria. Don't put words in my mouth. I think you would make a great addition to the staff on the ranch. I think you are more than capable of doing anything you want. I just want to make sure it's something that you want to do."

Gloria looked appeased for now and then went back into his arms. Reid held her close and tried not to let the little whispers of trepidation ease back into his soul. Whatever it was, he and Gloria would face it.

CHAPTER 6

*K*athy was once again at a loss for words. Just when she thought she knew Jack, he revealed something else about himself. She was already taken aback that he thought he wanted to be in any kind of relationship with her. He was forward, honest, and not as pushy as she thought he was going to be. All that put together, though, couldn't have prepared her for his statement.

"You were paralyzed at one time?"

"It's not something I bring up in common conversation, but you're not a common person," Jack said as the waitress cleared the table.

"Would the two of you like coffee?"

Kathy got ready to tell the waitress to go away when Jack beat her to the punch.

"If you could bring us both two coffees with some sugar and cream, that would be great," Jack said with a smile on his face but a tone that said they wanted some privacy. He did that so effortlessly. He took care of business without being rude, and it made her feel cared for in an odd way. Kathy hadn't felt cared for since her brother had found her, and he had to.

"How do you even know that I like coffee?" Kathy asked.

Jack smiled and leaned back in his chair.

"You looked in the sugar crate when I came in and pushed it to the side. I had a fifty-fifty chance that it was coffee and not tea. Besides, I was counting on fate not to let me be interested in a woman who likes tea."

Kathy thought he was incredulous, bold, and attractive all at the same time. No matter what happened, this night was one to remember.

"Okay, get on with your story because somehow I just can't imagine you paralyzed. You seem so…recovered."

"Isn't that the irony of it all? One day you can barely walk, and you are preparing for a life of learning how to live all over again. You meet people who are in the same situation that you are in, and for some reason, you get better, and others don't. It's a hard pill to swallow, and the guilt can eat you up, especially if you had begun to know the others who are still in that situation.

"I used to run a restaurant. It was my dream, actually. I had been open for maybe about a month, and everything was going well. The reviews were saying that it was the best food ever. I received compliments on the decor and the restaurant, and the presentation of the plates. I had even managed to have a relationship with the head chef, and the both of us were living our dreams.

"When a freak accident happened, it changed

everything. I was coming out of the kitchen one day, and there was something wet on the floor. Somehow, I managed to slip. Instead of falling directly on the floor, I hit the side of the counter in just the right place going down, and when I hit the floor, I felt nothing. In the beginning, everyone had said that it was just a shock. There was no real damage anyone could see at the time. But there was so much swelling that no one could really get a good look. Man, after about a week and I still couldn't move, a specialist came in and said that I was going to be paralyzed. Oh, they were going to do some operations if I wanted to do that, to see if it would work. But on the whole, these things either healed themselves or they didn't. And because it had already been a month, there was little hope.

"However, Gloria came. And even though I had given up, she hadn't."

"And your chef that you were having the relationship with?" Kathy couldn't stop herself from asking.

"When I fell, she took over the restaurant, and when it became too much for her, I agreed to sell, and she moved on."

"Ouch!"

"Yeah, I was really feeling low at the time, but I recovered. As a result, I get to indulge in my joy, and that is where I'm going tonight."

"I'm sorry I don't get the connection."

"When I was ill, I couldn't move or take care of things that brought me joy. I've always been a tinkerer, and I didn't leave the people I met when I was paralyzed. Instead, I decided that I would make things to help them out in their daily lives. A friend of mine lives nearby, and recently, he bought a dog. He's wheelchair-bound, but he wants to make sure he can care for his dog by himself and not the aide who comes by. I just finished the dog feeder, and I need to drop it by for him."

Kathy looked at Jack and was speechless. The night was turning into an in-depth look at Jack Danvers, and with every layer that was peeled back, Kathy found that she liked him more and more.

"I'd love to go with you to drop off the gift to your friend," Kathy said.

"Well, then I can stop stalling," Jack said as he called over the waitress. When the bill came, they both reached for it at the same time.

Jack shook his head. "I'm sorry. That is a no-go, princess. I said I was going to pay, and you said you were going to order the most expensive thing on the menu. I've seen the bill, and I have to say, you could have done better. Now, just because you were distracted by my good looks and charm doesn't mean I'm going to let you pay the bill," Jack said.

Kathy sputtered. "You're good looks and— You do have a healthy opinion about yourself, don't you?"

"To be honest, I didn't think I was all that great, but you've been looking at me all night with those gorgeous eyes, and now I have the confidence of ten men!"

"If I was looking into your eyes tonight, it's because I didn't realize you had such a good character."

"Wow, you know how to give it to a guy. I think I need to stop while I'm ahead, and we should go and see my friend," Jack joked.

"That's fine. I'll follow you. Just send me the address, and then we can both get on our way," Kathy said.

"Are we taking separate cars? I don't mind driving you there, and if you like, I can drive you back here to the restaurant to pick up your car."

Kathy gave him a sad smile and shook her head. "There are a couple of problems with your suggestion. The first one is I came here with the chauffeur, so it's not a matter of me driving at all. Second, a woman always makes sure she has her own transportation. You never know what's going to happen on a date."

Jack put his hands to his chest and opened his eyes wide. "Are you suggesting that I might do something? I mean, if I did, it would be poor planning. Everyone here has seen us, and this is a place where I know everyone. Doesn't seem like the way to go if I'm playing on doing something nefarious to you."

Kathy couldn't have agreed more, but she was sure that her brother would have the largest conniption if she came home in Jack's car. Tonight, was about living it up and dreaming big, not finding new ways to aggravate Reid.

Kathy held up her hands in front of her. "I hear, and I agree, but for tonight, let's just let things be, and I'll follow you."

Jack wasn't sure why he was nervous. He had been to see his friend Paul more times than he could count.

It was true that he was bringing Kathy, but that shouldn't have been a showstopper.

Jack already had the dog feeder in the back of his car. When Kathy's car showed up, he sat in his car waiting. This was the moment of truth. He had been so secure in it this morning, but now that Kathy was going to see it, maybe he should have painted it or made it look nicer. Paul's house was at the end of a cul-du-sac, and there wasn't much there by the way of lights. However, as soon as they pulled up, everyone would know he had a dog. Bella, the German shepherd, made no attempt to hide her presence. Kathy was already getting out of the car and meeting him at his vehicle.

"Well, it is very clear that he has a dog. We didn't talk about this before, but what exactly does Paul do?" Kathy asked with a smile.

"Do?"

"Yes, you know. What does he do to make money?" Kathy asked, exasperated.

"He's a dignity teacher," Jack said with no preamble.

"A dignity teacher?" Kathy asked. Jack could see that she was a little hesitant and wasn't clear on what a dignity teacher was.

"He teaches other people with disabilities how to live on their own. He has different levels of maintaining yourself, and it helps you to maintain your dignity. A lot of people have handicaps, but they don't necessarily need someone to do everything for them. These classes are for those people."

At first, Jack was a little worried because Kathy didn't say anything. However, as they got closer to the door, Kathy said, "What a great idea. To be a dignity coach."

The door opened, and a fit man in a neon yellow wheelchair met them at the door. Kathy walked up to him and shook his hand. "So, you're Paul. If I had known you were so handsome, I would have told Jack not to waste his money and that I'd have eyes just for you," Kathy said.

Paul laughed, shook her hand, and then winked at Jack. "Ah, I see you have a smart one here. She can recognize quality when she sees it." Then he turned to Kathy and wheeled his chair back so she could walk into the house.

"I'll be right there, Paul. I've got to get the feeder."

Jack went back to his car and got the feeder. As he was rolling it up into Paul's house, Jack could hear Paul saying, "Jack got me the refrigerator with the freezer at the bottom, and then he made a lot of compartments on my level so I could reach them. It works out great!" Paul was testifying.

When Jack walked in with the feeder, all eyes turned on him.

"Ah, It's about time. Bella is getting tired of being fed when the guy comes. You know kids are so flaky. Sometimes the boy shows up, and other times he's too busy with the girl who's going to leave him for a stable guy anyway," Paul cawed.

Kathy laughed and took a seat next to Paul. Paul started to talk to Kathy, and for once, he was very grateful. Jack couldn't tell anyone why he was so nervous. He had tested the feeder. He knew that it worked. Everything was just the way it was supposed to be. He called out for Bella. Not one to miss an opportunity to get food, Bella came patting along as soon as she heard Jack whistle for her.

"Don't be getting any ideas over there. Bella is my girl, and we've been through too much for me to even think about giving her up to you. No matter how cool you make things," Paul said, looking at Jack.

"Listen, I promise not to poach your girl. You promise not to poach mine, and we'll both get along just fine," Jack teased as Kathy laughed along with Paul.

"Well, I personally think that this girl should have some say in this matter," Kathy said heartily.

Jack glanced at Paul, and they both looked horrified. The men weren't quick enough, and Kathy caught their expressions.

"I won't even comment on that statement. Instead, let's see this feeder work!"

Jack moved out of the way and then turned to Paul.

"You can do the honors."

Paul moved his chair to the cabinet and then pulled out the bag of dog food and placed it in the open container of Jack's machine. Then Paul pushed a button, and the bottom was sliced open, and kibble fell into the tray. Without having to be asked twice, Bella came to the bowl to eat.

"Yes!" Paul said as he watched Bella eat. "This is exactly what I am looking for. Now you just need to get started on those other items, and we can start to talk about sharing them on a bigger scale."

Jack knew this was going to come up, and he had hoped he could avoid it with Kathy being here, but he was wrong.

"Paul, I don't mind making stuff for you, but for others? I don't know, I think it's just some scraps I put together. I couldn't in good conscience charge anyone because these are the scraps at my place."

Paul rolled up next to him and grabbed his arm. "I know you do this on the side, but consider how many others you could bring some dignity to. Just think about it."

Not wanting to overstay his welcome and definitely needing as much time as he could get with Kathy, Jack told Paul it was time for them to take their leave. When they got outside of Paul's house, Kathy's ride drove off.

He watched her walk to his car with a wide smile and then held open the door to his car. Jack was nervous when they pulled away, but he kept his hands on the wheel. Jack didn't want this night to end. He had already taken Kathy to see Paul. She seemed to enjoy herself while she was there, but still, it was an unusual place to go after a dinner date. Now that they were both in the car together, he found himself at a loss for words. How could he ask this woman to see him again when he hadn't exactly presented the best first date ever?

"Jack, I want to thank you for taking me to Paul's house."

"Well, it wasn't on the top ten places to take a date, but it was fun to see him, and I want to thank you for even going."

"Paul seems like good peeps," Kathy said.

"Remember what I said. Don't fall for the dog. I could get one in a minute."

Kathy laughed.

"So, when do we go out next time?" Jack asked.

"Next time?"

"I mean, you can't want to give up on us already?"

"Us? Wow, I didn't know there was an us."

"I know. That's why I'm here to help you out," Jack said.

"What would we do on our next date?"

"Does it matter?"

"Well, a woman wants to dress appropriately."

"I'm thinking we can go to a very small market and look at some really cool cheap goods and food. Again, I'll let you choose the cuisine," Jack said.

"Ah, so you are going the stomach route? Good idea. I have to say my stomach leads the way most of the time. Sooo since we've worked out the details, I'll meet you tomorrow?"

"Tomorrow it is. I'll send the name of the festival, and we can meet there and then you can decide if you need your chauffeur again."

Kathy smiled.

"I may have him drop me off. Will you give me a ride back?"

"I certainly will. Can't wait," Jack said as they pulled up in front of Reid's place.

Jack got out and opened her door.

"It's been a pleasure," he said to Kathy.

"No, the pleasure was all mine, and I hope to continue it tomorrow." Jack thought about giving her a peck on the cheek, but then he saw Reid at the door. "Well, I'd better leave before your chaperone gets me," he joked.

Kathy looked at the door and hung her head. "I'm sorry," she murmured, embarrassed.

"Don't be. Good things are worth the wait. Go,

princess. I'll see you tomorrow." Resigned, Kathy left, and Jack watched her go into her home. It was funny. When you weren't looking for answers, they just showed up and said, here I am. Jack just hoped he was ready.

CHAPTER 7

*K*athy's day wasn't going the way she wanted it to go. She had to cancel her date with Jack because she had been summoned by Mr. Dane for lunch. Reid was acting strange and wouldn't discuss it. Unfortunately, Kathy didn't have the patience to listen. She hadn't realized how much she had been looking forward to meeting Jack today.

What she should have done was cancel with Mr. Dane, but it was too late when she was sitting at the table waiting for Mr. Dane to arrive. Then, on time, as usual, Mr. Dane showed up. He took three seconds before he jumped right into the matter.

"So, what has upset you? I haven't even spoken yet," Mr. Dane said.

Was he always this intuitive, or was it just after Patti had passed?

"Forgive me, but I find our meetings always leave me with very little to be happy about."

"I'm sorry you feel that way. I'm just trying to make sure that all that Patti wanted comes to pass."

Kathy looked at Mr. Dane and had to take a second look at his motivations. Maybe they had all been too tied up in the pain of losing Patti that they hadn't seen how her passing had affected Mr. Dane. Kathy wanted to be sympathetic, but every time she turned around, it just seemed like Mr. Dane was in the midst of things, and they were never going well.

"Reid missed the corporate meeting last week. Does this mean he's—"

"It doesn't mean anything except that he needs to look at his calendar more often."

Mr. Dane looked as though he were about to say something, and then he shook his head in consternation.

"Last quarter's numbers are up, and we are taking on three more companies."

"Yes, it does seem like things are moving along, despite Reid's preoccupation with other endeavors. I was surprised you were in the bay," Mr. Dane said. So, this was the moment of truth. The real reason that Mr. Dane wanted to see Kathy was to find out what had brought her to Inheritance Bay.

"I still have friends here that I would like to see, especially after Miss Patti's passing."

"Of course," Mr. Dane said.

Kathy couldn't tell why, but there was a pregnant pause where she was just waiting for it all to fall free. "I had a meeting with Jack Danvers if you must know."

Mr. Dane was not pleased.

"Is there a problem, Mr. Dane?" Kathy asked, surprised to see a reaction from Mr. Dane.

"There isn't a problem. I just thought that when

you decided to go back into the dating world, it would have been with someone in the same field, perhaps."

Kathy smiled. "Jack and I are in the same field —business."

Mr. Dane nodded and then let out a sigh. "I suppose you are right. Again, forgive me for being a bit protective. It's one of the last things left to me. I've watched you grow up into a smart, attractive woman, and I just want to make sure you are around men who are deserving of you."

Kathy sat back and looked at Mr. Dane. He was a bit red around the collar, and if she didn't know any better, she might have thought Mr. Dane was uncomfortable with the subject.

"We've talked about that. I would like to talk about something else that is very important. I'm sure it doesn't even need to be said, but you know how I like to make sure all of the ends are tied up nice and neat."

Kathy could tell she already wasn't going to like this. Just when she thought she had seen a sliver of humanity from Mr. Dane, all of a sudden, it was gone. And here he was, the Mr. Dane she knew.

"I can't imagine what you could have left to chance."

Mr. Dane reached into his jacket pocket and pulled out a couple of papers.

"Patty had this made up while she was living, and I never really understood it, but she seemed to be very adamant about it. Now that she has passed on, I think it's only fair to give you a copy of it."

The sense of dread was circling Kathy. Her

breathing was becoming shallow, and for some reason, it seemed as though it was getting hotter.

"You're making this sound very ominous, Mr. Dane," Kathy said as she took the papers from his hand.

Mr. Dane waved off the words. "Ominous? No, no, dear. I don't think that this should be ominous at all. Patti was very determined to tie you and Reid together. As a result, she had these papers drawn up."

"Together?" Kathy echoed as she read through the papers. As she went on, she couldn't believe what she was reading.

"Mr. Dane, there must be some mistake, or there has to be some way to undo this!"

Mr. Dane shook his head and looked at her as if she were not well. "It wasn't a mistake. This is exactly what Patty wanted before she passed away. She was very clear that these were the terms, and Reid had already agreed to it."

"What do you mean? Reid had already agreed to it?"

Mr. Dane looked at her and splayed his hands out as if in supplication. "Reid agreed that whatever it is the both of you had should be fifty-fifty. When Reid made Patty a part owner of all of his assets, she became an equal business partner. She was concerned someone might try to kidnap or take the other one, so Reid agreed to these terms."

"These terms say that if one of us disappears, that the remaining party will be given a settlement, and the rest of the money will go to charity," Kathy said in disbelief.

"Yes, essentially that is it. Patti saw all of you making money, and she didn't want someone to disappear or for you all to break up. She wanted to make sure you all stayed close and were family. The only one who has an exclusion was Quinn, for obvious reasons."

Kathy looked at the papers again and just let it sink in. Patti knew her. Patti knew what she was going to do before she did it, like all good mothers did. The rest of the lunch was a blur. The carefully laid plans she had were laid to waste by the love of her mother. It was odd that she didn't feel as bad as she thought she would. It was still a shock, but she had decided to go to Reid's local office to work as she digested that she wasn't going anywhere.

It was funny how things worked together. For lunch, Mr. Dane had delivered her a wrench in her plans, and then a knock on her door, and whom should it be, but Jack Danvers behind a bouquet of roses.

Kathy was completely amazed how Jack could let himself act as if they were two high school students, with him being totally infatuated. His head poked around the corner, and then the roses appeared right below his chin. His eyes were bright, and his smile was as wide as the cat who had caught the mouse. Not even waiting for an invitation, he strode into her office and sat down.

It was then that Kathy was reminded that she was on a business call. Jack stood up and looked around like he was taking inventory of the office, examining every picture and every knick-knack on the shelves. He must have been the child who couldn't refrain from touching everything. When the call was finally done, Kathy tried to compose herself before she turned her chair to face him.

"If this is a waiting game, I could do this, but it's not as fun as talking to each other," he said.

She tried not to smile. Encouraging the bad behavior would only make it worse, but there was something so pure and refreshing about Jack's attraction to her.

"I am not playing a game. I'm trying to be the adult in the room," she said in slow, measured breaths.

"Well, it sounds like you aren't going to have any fun. I brought you flowers so you would smile, and I could see the sunrise again."

Kathy's heart sped up, and her blood pumped faster. When was the last time she had received a compliment that was about her and not her skill set? She turned around and gave him a tremulous smile.

"Okay, maybe not a sunrise but more sunset?" Jack said with a laugh.

"You are always so relaxed."

"I have to be. If I were uptight all the time, the stress might kill me," Jack said. "It's about choices."

"Choices, you say?"

"Yes, like you have a choice if you want to go out to dinner with me. I normally wouldn't ask, but the plans we had for today were thrown away after I prepped for our date."

Kathy looked at him, and she wasn't buying it. "You prepped for our date?"

"Ah! I see the look of disbelief in your eyes! Of

course, I prepped for our date. I had to hunt for new cuisine but still, keep us to the cover of darkness. Then there was the practicing at the Claw house. I had to ask every woman who came by what they thought would be a good gift for you, and that was how I came up with the roses!"

Kathy started laughing then. "You asked all the women what to get me?"

"Yes. I have to tell you it was perilous. Some of them thought I meant them, but I told them no, I was really trying to get the best present for my date."

"I can see the danger you faced," she said. "Is that why you are here to ask me to dinner?"

"No, I'm here to return the favor."

"Return the favor?" Kathy asked lost.

"Yes, I'm here to do some yelling of my own."

"Oh! And what would you be yelling at me about?"

"Well, I think you were waiting for any reason to cancel today because I wanted to go to a fair. Admit it. You didn't want to go."

Kathy thought about all of the other valid reasons she could have given him but decided she wouldn't.

"You're right. I didn't want to go."

"You can't just ditch me when you don't want to do something. Imagine how lost and lonely I could be."

"One, you were right I didn't want to go. I don't know about the other stuff, but you have the right to be mad."

"Woo hoo! Well, now that's over, let's go do a makeup dinner. I know this place you're going to love."

Kathy watched Jack jump up and offer his arm. Then Kathy thought about what Jack had said. Life was about choices, and she was going to make some for herself. With that resolve, she twined her arm in Jack's and hoped she wouldn't regret it.

CHAPTER 8

*J*ack helped Kathy to come out of the car and then pulled her into his embrace.

"Yes?" Kathy said.

"It's only us two. You can tell me. I'm growing on you, aren't I?"

He watched her smile at him.

"Fungus grows on things, so I'm not sure that is what you are looking for?"

Jack smiled back. "You know, some fungus is really good and helps people get well."

"You are impossible! Feed me as you promised me."

"Yes, my lady. I know not to get in between you and your food."

"Smart man, now let's get me fed. What is this?"

Jack let Kathy go and then guided her into The Silver Pond.

"It's a Dim Sum house. However, what makes this place special is that the small plates are from different cuisines. I think you'll like it."

The waitress guided them to a table in the corner, and Jack could see Kathy relax as they closer they got to their destination. After they were seated, Jack tapped the waitress on the arm.

"Yes?" the waitress replied.

"We're doing the chef special sampler."

The waitress's eyes lit up, and she shuffled away.

"So, is supposed to be a part of your charm?" Kathy asked.

For a moment, Jack thought he had done something wrong, but when he looked into Kathy's eyes, he could see she had a twinkle of mischievousness shining back at him.

"The sampler is a little bit of everything on the menu. I didn't want you to have to pick.. Besides, I noticed the last time we were out, you were having some problems spending money, and I wanted to take that responsibility off of your shoulders and order the most expensive thing on the menu. That would be the other reason why the waitress was so happy because she is thinking about her tip."

"You clearly have been here before, and it bodes well for you that they like you," Kathy said. "I'm actually surprised at how well-known you are in these different places. I would assume that you wouldn't frequent these spots because you obviously know how to cook."

"You are right. I do know how to cook. The problem is, I don't like cooking just for one person, and sometimes I get tired of my own cooking."

"So, you come here? By yourself?"

"Don't make it sound so sad. I have to tell you that I spend the majority of my day being surrounded by people in the park. Having a little peace and quiet isn't so bad."

"So help me figure this out, Jack. At one time, you had a restaurant, and everything was going well, and then you hit a hardship that you overcame. How does overcoming that hardship land you with the food truck in the park?"

"When I first opened up the truck, it was to get over a couple of fears that I had developed. While I was walking again and everything seemed like it was going well, there was always this little fear in the back of my mind that I would slip on something again and I would be paralyzed again. In the beginning, the truck was just about giving me a small space for me to be able to cook so I would have more control of my environment. Then I discovered I really do like talking to people one-on-one. Running a restaurant is a huge responsibility. People don't realize you don't have as much time in the front as you probably like. The truck lets me get to know everyone as a person and even to know what they really like so when they show up again; I can have it ready when they get there. In the beginning, it was a crutch, and now it's a lifesaver."

"You don't miss the glitz and the large kitchen and hearing all the pots and pans clatter with the latest equipment?"

"No, actually. I don't miss it at all. I feel like I live a fuller life now than I did then. I'm not saying that everything was bad about that life. I'm just saying I'm not there anymore."

"What about the work that you do with your friends like Paul?"

"That's not work. That's me giving back to those who were there for me."

"You seem almost seem to be too good of a guy, Jack," Kathy said.

"I'm not one to be put on a pedestal. I'm just someone who fell and realized what was important in life. I realize that people are important."

"People can be fickle," Kathy said in a small voice. Kathy was likely speaking from experience and not pessimism. He reached his hand out and covered hers on the table.

"People are individuals. Some people are good, and some are not, but what's important is that we keep ourselves open and give them all a chance."

"You believe that? If after you've been hurt, you still think they deserve a chance?"

Jack leaned closer to her across the table.

"I think that, especially after what I've gone through. Some people weren't too good for me."

"This I've got to hear," Kathy said sarcastically.

"Well, my thought is this. People come in egg cartons."

Kathy snorted just as the waitress was bringing water and the first courses. After the waitress had left the items on the plate, she looked at him, trying not to smile.

"Okay, would you like to try that again?"

"Yes, listen, this is great wisdom. People are like eggs in a carton. It's true that one or two might not be good, and a couple might even be cracked. However, if you've run into all of the bad ones, then you are on your way to getting to the good ones."

Kathy looked at him with her mouth open as he popped the first potsticker in his mouth.

"I think you should eat and not hang your mouth like that. It will be our luck a reporter catches a picture of you like that," Jack said. Her mouth immediately closed.

"What happens when the whole dozen is bad?"

Jack smiled. "I haven't found an egg carton like that in all of my life. One of them will pass muster."

"I don't know about this Pollyanna attitude, Jack."

"Don't worry. It'll rub off on you." Kathy started eating, looking at him speculatively. It was the first time in a while that Jack hoped what he was saying was true. He certainly hoped he was starting to rub off on Kathy because, as he spent more time with her, he was beginning to realize she was becoming the one for him.

Grayson Chance was a man in love. He had married his true love Rose, and now they lived in his adopted mom, Patti's, house. It was still hard to believe that his mom had passed away. Grayson always thought he would have more time. More time to spend with his mother and more time for her to meet the love of his life. In the end, it turned out he didn't have either. His mother used to always say, "You have to go through the sorrowful times to appreciate and understand the good times." Grayson laughed to himself, remembering how silly he used to think that statement was. Now that he was married to a woman he absolutely adored and had the twins in his life, he got it. As usual, his mother was right.

"Grayson, I really need to talk to you." Rose

Chance rushed into his office and the feeling of being beyond fortunate flooded Grayson. At 5'8 with her hair in a ball, she was a whirlwind. The twins kept them both on their toes, and Grayson was glad that they had both learned to trust each other and marry.

"Yes, Rose," he said, moving aside the files he was looking at on potential fundraisers he might do. Everyone wanted him to run a fundraiser for them. With his connections to the philanthropic and his brothers who were rich or close to it in their own right, when Grayson Chance threw a fundraiser, checks would be written.

Rose took a seat in front of his desk and started to nibble her bottom lip. Whatever it was, it was big.

"Go ahead, love."

After his urging, her face relaxed, and she gave him a smile that would move him to give her whatever she desired.

"Grayson, I just found out something, and I have to admit I'm a bit nervous."

"Because—?"

"We talk about everything, and this wasn't one of those things."

Grayson waited. He loved Rose, but she could get upset about small things easily. He knew it was because she was so considerate of everyone else.

"Tell me, Rose. We can handle it together," he said in a low voice.

"I hope so because we're married, and I'm not letting you go."

"Well, that is a reason as well. Go ahead, Rose."

"Well, what I want to say is—"

"Yes—"

Rose squirmed in her seat.

"I mean, I've been trying to say this to you all week actually and—"

"And?"

"Well—"

"I love you, Rose. Spit it out!" he said.

"I'm pregnant!" she shouted. Just like that, silence blanketed the office.

"You're pregnant?"

"Yes, pregnant. Your thoughts?"

Thoughts? Who had thoughts now? He knew what had to be done. He stood up and pulled Rose into his arms.

"I don't know why you waited so long to tell me! Another baby is a gift," he said as he whispered the words into her hair.

"Are you okay with this, Grayson?"

"Yes, I am." He pulled back and looked at her. "Well, I don't see any changes yet. No horns are growing out of your head yet, but there's still time," Grayson joked.

Rose fell against him in relief. "I was nervous, Grayson. We were just married. The twins are still finding their way in school this year and—"

"And we'll get through this together. The baby will bring its own personality, and we will be better for it."

Rose looked up at him and then kissed him. "Thank you for being so amazing! I've got to go and tell the others. I wanted to tell you first."

Grayson watched Rose leave just as quickly as she came, and then he fell into the nearest seat.

Oh, my goodness, another child. The twins were going to kill him, and now the new baby would just put him in a grave. Grayson was going to have to find a way to deal with this new life. He was happy and horrified all at the same time. They had just gotten married, and …. Grayson knew what he had to do. He reached for his phone and did the only thing he could.

"Hey, I wanted to know if the guys could come out for dinner. I've got news."

CHAPTER 9

*K*athy hadn't slept very well at all. She dreamt about eggs in egg cartons. Every egg in the carton jumped up. One needed to say that it was a good egg. There were even a couple of eggs in the carton that were cracked they tried to speak up as well. All in all, it made for a restless night. Kathy was back in the office and trying to go over some reports. The problem was, every time she looked at the reports, she thought about Jack. Then as if thoughts alone could conjure him up, there was a knock on her door.

"Hello?"

"If you're here, who's running the truck?" Kathy asked.

"Fortunately, I have friends who don't mind filling in for me while I go on an extended lunch," Jack said with a smile on his face.

"These must be friends who really like you because this is the second day that you're playing hooky."

"Why, hooky is such a negative connotation. I'm investing in my future," Jack said.

Kathy looked at him and realized he was. Mr. Dane's news had put a cramp in her leaving like she planned, but there were other ways to be out of the way. Jack was amazing. In fact, Kathy still had a hard time understanding why Jack was around her at all.

"I was wondering what you were doing later. I didn't want you to have to come to the park. I understand how irresistible I can be, and so I came here."

"Did you?" Kathy confirmed. "Well, I can't say that I had the overwhelming urge to go to the park and seek you out."

"What?" Jack said in mock offense. "No worries, it will come. I can assure you," Jack said as he leaned on her desk and gave her an outrageous smile.

"You know, if a sparkle happens to appear on your front two teeth, I'm going to jump away completely scared that you are a cartoon character."

Jack waved off the concern. "Let's talk about what's important. Tell me, did you like the smell of my new soap?"

Kathy was confused, and then she took a deep breath.

"I can't really smell anything but…"

"Then it's working. I ran out of detergent last night and had to hand wash my truck shirt. I couldn't even find the other one. I think what I need is a person, not male, to pick up some supplies."

"Really? Maybe you should just order what you need online and go back to building those projects for your friends."

"I can go back to those projects later."

"Hmm. I don't know. I think your friends really depend on you, and I think your time would be better spent doing that rather than hanging out here," Kathy said.

Jack's smile slipped, and he gave her an odd look.

"My friends understand that it takes some time for me to build things," he said.

Kathy pushed back from her desk and sighed. "Maybe it's not my place to say."

"Kathy, please. You can say anything between us," Jack said, coming into the office and closing the door.

"I just think they are all counting on you, and you are here with me, joking around and flirting in a game. You could be doing really good with them. If I were you, I'd be thrilled that I could help someone."

Kathy saw Jack take a step back, and she knew she had said the wrong thing. It didn't come out right, but Kathy couldn't think of anything better than to be able to help other people. She helped Reid, but what Jack did could help hundreds or thousands of people at once.

"I'm sorry, Jack. It seems like I've overstepped and—"

"No, you are telling the truth as you see it. I mean, you don't know all of the facts of what and when I do, but—"

Kathy stood up and went to Jack. "You're right. I have no right to say anything one way or another. I don't know a lot about it. It was just a thought. As I said, you have such a great effect on so many people with the work that you do."

Jack nodded and then backed up.

"I thought I was having an effect on you two, Kathy."

Kathy looked at him, and everything in her wanted to go to him and say yes, he was making her think about her life, but then she realized this was probably the best time to stop living in this la-la land. Jack had purpose to others, and he was kind and humble. He was just a great all-around person. She, on the other hand, was trying to get her bearings. She had a plan last week that was gone now. She had to think of what she was going to do. Eventually, Reid would be completely vested in the ranch, and Gloria could do what she did. Yes, this was the best option.

Taking her seat back on the other side of her desk, she placed her hands on top of the desk and pulled some files open.

"Look, I shouldn't have said anything. What you do with your time is your own business," Kathy finished abruptly.

"If that is the way you feel about it."

Kathy shuffled the papers in front of her, not seeing them. She had started down this path, hoping to show him how special he was and how needed, and now there were words that made no sense and couldn't be brought back.

"So, I take it you're going to be busy later?" Jack said. Kathy couldn't imagine sitting at a table with this awkwardness. She glanced up to see him looking at her, confused and hurt.

"I'm sorry, I have to finish up some reports for Mr. Dane. They were due a couple of days ago, but I hadn't gotten to them."

"No worries. I've got to get back to the truck."

Kathy understood how he was needed by his friends and by the truck and the people in the park, and she was just here to fix papers for Reid. Kathy really thought about her life and what she did. Jack probably saw what she saw. She didn't contribute to a group of people like he did. She didn't serve anyone or get to know anyone as he did in the park. In fact, he probably saw that she was a one-trick pony. She didn't even have hobbies that helped anyone. All this time, she had been worried about Jack. Kathy now saw there was no need. Jack had a life, and he didn't live in a bubble, and he wasn't afraid to live life to the fullest, even though bad things had happened.

"Should I come by truck? I can help you take some more things over to Paul...maybe," she said in a low voice. Say something, Kathy thought. Kathy was internally pleading for it not to end like this.

Jack straightened his back and smiled. "I've got to catch up on truck business. I don't need any help to do that." Then he turned and walked out. Kathy watched him walk out the door, and even after he was gone, she still looked at the door. Maybe he would come back and say they should meet. Maybe he would say.... something. Ten minutes passed, and Jack didn't return. Kathy thought she had experienced being alone, but this was worse than any other time. It was worse because Kathy thought she was the cause of this pain to herself, and she had no idea how to fix it.

~

～

There was no rest for the wicked, slow, or dumb. Kathy had heard that expression from one of the families that had fostered her. She knew it was true but just didn't know which category she was today.

With a smile that was too bright and a ponytail that bounced behind her, Kathy watched as Traci came into her office. She should have expected that this was going to happen sooner or later, especially after the phone call.

"Kathy, I'm glad that I caught you here. I was trying to find the right time to come and see you," Traci said as she took a seat in front of Kathy's desk.

"Really, Traci. I don't know that we really have anything to talk about."

Kathy could see that that wasn't the answer that Traci was waiting for. The last time that Kathy had seen Traci was at her wedding. Everyone was shocked when Vincent said he wanted to get married. He was the suspicious brother, if ever there was one. No matter how nice his previous relationships had seemed, Vincent had found a way to sabotage it or investigate them until something unsavory came out of their past.

To be honest, Kathy was a little disappointed that she had found Traci at the clinic. It would be one of those things that Vincent would count as a deception to split. However, she was the last one to judge. Somehow, she had managed to push away an amazing man, and she wasn't even sure how it had happened.

"I think we do have something to talk about. I'm

going to talk to Vincent, but I didn't think it made sense to talk to him if nothing was possible."

Kathy looked at Traci, confused. "You have a child already. I would think that would be enough confirmation that you can have a child."

Traci looked uncomfortable and then let out a big breath.

"The question isn't, can I have a child. The question is, can I have a child that doesn't have any genetic or hereditary diseases," she said in a low slow voice.

Kathy sat back in her chair and looked at Traci. It had never occurred to her it would matter. Kathy thought she must have been quiet for too long because Traci spoke up to fill the void.

"The question is not about keeping the baby. That is already a given for us. The question is how much preparation it will take. Should we wait until Sophia is older so I can handle a child that may need more from me? Vincent is running a company and doing what he loves. I am finally doing what I love. Vincent can provide so I don't need to choose one or the other. However, I want to be fair to the children we would have. I want to make sure I can be there for them like they may need."

Kathy felt ashamed. She had jumped to the wrong conclusion, and she knew Traci. She could only imagine how she had jumped to the wrong conclusion about Jack as well. Kathy leaned forward and placed her hand on top of Traci's.

"Listen, it's not my play, either way, to say what should or shouldn't be. The only piece of advice I'd like to give is the piece I'm going to take myself. Be open and honest with him. Say exactly what you mean so there are no misunderstandings. The most important thing is that he hears it from your mouth first."

Traci smiled. "I will. I'm going to tell him about this week on our date night. I don't know if he'll every want to date me again, but I will bring it up."

Kathy smiled and sat down. "He'll date you again. He just may ask for an agenda for your next date," Kathy said as both women laughed.

CHAPTER 10

"What is going on with the women in my life?" Reid asked as Kathy put the phone to her ear.

"It's almost the end of the day, and I thought maybe, just maybe, I'd be able to make it home in time to do a little self-care," she mumbled.

"When did we start keeping secrets from each other?" Reid asked.

"Reid?"

"Kathy," Reid continued barreling on with good intent. "I hear that Jack has been coming by the office almost every day."

Kathy let her head fall onto her desk. She had only been here a couple of days, and somehow it turned from two days to a lifetime of Jack seeing her.

"Really? Really is that what you really want to talk to me about?"

"I think that's the point, Kathy. We are not talking. The waitress at one of the restaurants

85

happens to be the daughter of one of the people I know who said to me in passing; it's so nice to see your sister is out and about. Man, I go ahead and call your office only to find out that my sister is indeed out and about for the second day in a row with the same man."

"Would you have preferred if it had been a different man? Would that have made any difference?"

"First of all, the problem is Jack is not a real man. Jack is Gloria's brother that makes him barely human. On top of it all, I was waiting for you to start dating so I could go around and intimidate your new guy. Make sure he treats you right. All of that payback goes right out the door with Jack."

"Can you explain to me exactly why you're upset? Is it because you think I'm keeping secrets or because I went out and had lunch and dinner with Jack?"

"Lunch and dinner. Wow, I'm really behind the times here. And when were you going to let me know any of this?"

"I think I did tell you that I was going to dinner with Jack, but I don't think he really registered with you all that much. Then on the night that I went out to dinner, I was running late, and I told you about it then."

"You've been seeing him since that night?"

Kathy couldn't believe he was making such a big deal out of this. "The last time I checked, I was a big girl, and I'm in the town of Inheritance Bay. The small town where no one sleeps because they might miss someone else doing something. What's the problem?"

Reid groaned on the other end. "I don't have a problem."

"We can agree or disagree that you don't have a problem right now. The truth is you're unhappy with the situation. Do you have a reason for that?" Kathy asked.

"I don't need a reason. I'm your brother," Reid complained. "No one will ever be good enough for you. I want to protect you from all the things that might cause you not to smile. Shouldn't you trust me when I say he's not good enough?"

"Maybe I should be asking you what kind of questions you've been asking that people think that it's okay to run back to you and tell you who I'm with."

"Anyone who knows me knows how much I love and adore you. I couldn't be happier that you're getting out now, but I want to make sure that you're okay. Does that mean that people may come back to me and say, hey, you're with someone A or B, or you're walking down the street? Maybe. I don't know. That's really a part of them trying to keep an eye on you as much as it is a part of being in a small nosy town."

Kathy sighed and then tried to let the tension go. This was such a moot conversation, anyway. This just emphasized how she had just messed up due to... She couldn't even name it.

"Stop stressing, Reid. Nothing is going to come of this, okay? So, you don't have to go all hero mode and hunt down Jack."

"Did he hurt you?"

Kathy didn't know what to say to her brother. There was nothing that she could say without giving too much detail, and at the end of the day, it wasn't even Jack's fault.

"I'm not appreciating the silent treatment right now, Kathy."

"Give me some space while I try to work this out. Okay? The problem here isn't Jack. I'm pretty sure the issue here is me."

Kathy sat back in her chair and let her head fall onto the headrest. Her eyes closed, and she tried to fend off the burning behind her eyelids.

"Kat, do you need me to get you? We can go hang out, and I'll provide a dart board with his face on it. I just happen to have one handy," Reid said solemnly.

Kathy laughed through the grief. "You just happen to have one around?"

"It was a novelty item. I was just practicing," Reid defended.

"I wouldn't do that to him. Not even a picture of him."

"Ugh! I don't want to say I told you so, but …. This guy isn't even worthy of being on the same field as you," Reid muttered.

"Not worthy? What are you kidding me?"

"He can't take care of you in the fashion you are accustomed to. He runs a truck, for goodness's sake. It would be one thing if he didn't know how to do better, but he chooses to run a truck instead of a real business. It just shows that he's lazy and he's not good enough for you."

"You know, Reid, you are absolutely right. That should definitely be one of my life goals after growing up in the foster care system to go and find someone who makes just as much money or more than I make, even though I can't even spend the money that we make right now. And that truck, I can see that that's really bothering you. But you know what? That truck is a real business, and it's more grassroots than what we are. He knows exactly what's going on and when it's going on, when the people's taste changed, and how. I wish we could say we had that much insight into what was going on and to some of our businesses on the ground floor."

"Maybe that's the problem, Kathy. Hey, maybe you're right, and he is the next Mother Teresa, but in a man form. I have to tell you something. Being a man, it might be a little tough to be next to a woman. I'm always going to be suspected of marrying her for her money and being second best."

"Jack wouldn't care. That is what is so special about him. He wouldn't care what others thought. Did you know he was an inventor?"

"What did you say?"

"I said that he does amazing things with his hands and …"

Reid guffawed on the other end.

"Wait, wait, wait for it. Are you trying to tell me that Mr. No Restaurant In a Food Truck is also a handyman that makes junk workable?"

Kathy just wanted to reach into the phone and shake some sense into Reid.

"That's what got him upset. I think I sounded like a snob, and I didn't mean to."

"Kathy, you've got to be overthinking this. You could never sound like a snob."

"You don't understand. That thing that he does

making stuff is for people who are disabled. I told him maybe he should be spending more time doing that and doing something meaningful rather than working at that truck."

"Ouch!"

"You are not helping this, by the way."

For the next few minutes, the only thing that could be heard on the phone was Kathy and Reid breathing.

"Reid? Don't leave me hanging now."

"The question here is, were you serious? Did you mean it?"

"I think at the time I said it I thought the things he made with his hands were more important. I thought the things that he left behind would have been more important than the people who just passed by on the truck."

"Did Jack share with you that he made stuff by hand, or did you discover it on your own?"

"He shared it with me."

She heard Reid grunt again on the other line.

"You are really bad at this, Reid," Kathy complained.

"Well, I'm not a fan of the guy, but some basics have been breached here and I think it's important that you think about them. If you really believe what you said, then there is no way to fix it. Just go your way and let him find himself and heal up."

"Heal up?"

"I don't know why he runs the truck, but the truth of it is no one wants to be told they are doing something useless. I don't know why he builds the things with his hands either, but he does, and if he invited you into that, then you just went in and passed judgment."

"Don't you think I know that? That's why I said that's what I thought, but I know better now. I can see beyond the shallowness of the dollar right now and see that there are other things that are more important. He's not here, though. I let him walk out of the door because I didn't want to say anything or…. I don't even know why I let him walk out of the door, but he's gone."

"I can have him back in your office if you just say the word," Reid promised like any good overbearing brother would.

That was how it normally worked. If Kathy had a problem and she couldn't solve it, she knew her brother would come to her aid. She thought of the good times that she had with Jack at the restaurant over dinner and even talked over silly things. He was so different than every other person that she had met. She knew it was its own form of self-sabotage that had made her say those things without thought. More importantly, it was the self-sabotage that kept her from going after him.

Kathy was so conflicted. She wanted to run back and throw herself at Jack's feet and say she was sorry for being a snob, but at the same time, she wanted Jack to understand and to come back.

"You don't need to hunt him down. I think you and I should meet up."

"You want to meet up with your brother now? I'm honored. My offer is still going to stand tomorrow, so sleep on it and think about it. Your happiness is all that matters, and I will bring him back to you," Reid promised.

"No, silly. Stop blustering, and I'll talk to you soon."

Kathy put the phone down and then looked out her office window. If only life was that simple, and Reid could just bring Jack back to her.

CHAPTER 11

*M*eet at the usual spot?

Jack glanced at the text from his sister Gloria. This meeting was going to be happening sooner or later. He wasn't sure how long it would take for Kathy to go home and see her brother, but he knew that when her brother saw her, he would tell Gloria.

It had always been their practice that whenever one of them wanted to talk, they would find a neutral area so that both of them could walk away. They both had solid opinions, and it was best to walk away and come back then to stay and say something you couldn't take back.

It seemed as though today was going to be one of those types of conversations. Sitting on the bench, not even twenty feet away from his truck, he waited for his sister. She was dressed in her ever-comfortable blue jeans and basic white shirt. Jack was always amazed at how Gloria could be wearing white in the planning business, where she had to scout sites, go to new places, and evaluate dusty computer rooms. Somehow, she managed never to get her shirts dirty. He, on the other hand, tried to make sure all of his shirts were dark because it was only a matter of time before something spilled on them. He knew firsthand that butter stained just as much as the red sauce. And since he ran a truck called the Claw House, there was lots of butter involved. Yes, this was going to be a doozy of a conversation.

"I'm loving that white shirt you're rocking today," Jack said without preamble.

"You're just jealous."

"That doesn't negate my first statement at all. It's still a great shirt."

"You know. I know that I said that I wanted the both of us to get out more and do things and meet new people, but I have to tell you, I never thought the new people you would include on your list would be Kathy."

"To be fair, I'd have to tell you I would have also been in that same boat. Sometimes we don't get to pick whom we go with or whom we don't. We just have chemistry, and it goes from there."

Gloria smiled and then turned to face her brother. "Chemistry. Is that what we're calling it these days?"

Jack couldn't resist reaching out and tugging on a strand of hair that was behind her ear.

"You know, Jack, I'm not five years old anymore. Tugging my hair won't distract me from the purpose of this meeting."

"Just what is the purpose of this meeting because I have to tell you I'm a little confused."

"Really? You're dating Kathy!"

"Is that what she said? And don't women do that all the time in this day and age?" Jack asked with a bemused expression on his face.

"Of course, women date. The routine is, a sister dates, and then the guy who wants to be in her life gets vetted by her brother or some other such archaic practice," Gloria said, shaking her head in confusion.

"Well, I don't remember that, and I'm pretty sure I'm a brother."

"Yes, well…"

"When you were dating Reid, I thought you had enough smarts and common sense for me not to interfere unless it looked like you were floundering. Is that what happened? Did Reid think Kathy looked like she needed help?"

"No."

"Okay, then what is the problem?" Jack asked, trying to keep his tone even and not be upset by this mini inquisition. Kathy was an amazing woman. Despite not having a stable child life, she had managed to still be a kind woman. Her ability to help Reid out was just fascinating to him. He knew she didn't do public, but he didn't see that as a real barrier until now. He had thought her staying inside was more about being stalked for her money than her. Had he misjudged the situation?

If he were honest with himself, he would have to say that the real problem was she had called him out on doing more for his friends. He wanted to do more but he didn't want to talk about his path and how they all met. It seemed like his past was always going to haunt him. When he came to Inheritance Bay, he wanted a new start. He couldn't talk about the work he did without bringing up how he had another life and how shallow he was. It was in such sharp contrast to the man he was today that he wasn't sure the good people of Inheritance Bay would be able to reconcile it.

Maybe Kathy had the same problem. Maybe she thought that people had one view of her, and she wanted to do something more but didn't know what. Jack had to admit he had been wracking his head to try and find out what the problem was.

"In other news, I've decided that I want to be a therapist," Gloria said.

Jack stopped and looked at his sister. He could see it, but it was a big jump.

"I hear there is a lot of schooling involved. If my memory serves me right, that is not your favorite place to be."

Gloria shrugged. "We're married now, and I want to do more. Something with Reid."

"You are the most organized person I know. You do yoga, you know finance, and you can put anything in order. You're a great person, Gloria."

He saw her nod and then go on. "Those things are nice, but I need some purpose in my life and I want to do something that Reid and I can do together. Yoga is great and now finishing up the studio isn't a problem, but I want to help those who have a real need, I guess. Anyway, I have said my piece and told you about my new life plan. The only thing left to tell you is that Kathy is already at the house with Reid."

"What? I think maybe you should have led the whole conversation with that statement."

Gloria gave him a long look. And then tsked, tsked. "You obviously have not been in the dating game very long at all. Otherwise, you would know I have to have some loyalty to my own gender first. Also, you are really head over heels for this, aren't you?"

Jack held up his hands and took a deep breath.

"You know I care for you, Gloria, but I don't need the sermon right now. I just need to know why is she here? Did she say?"

"You mean you want to know whether or not she's coming to see you? I have no clue. However, just take a hint from another woman when I say don't let misunderstandings get in the way. If there's something you want to tell her, just go to her."

Gloria's words rattled around in Jack's head after she left. After he got the second customer's order wrong, he told the college guy who was helping him today he was going to leave early. The help was thrilled. When Jack wasn't in the truck with him, he made two dollars more an hour. Jack couldn't even focus on the uptick in salary. He needed to go work with his hands. He needed the garage.

Who knew that cutlery could be so tricky? Jack checked his e-mail and found there were several more requests that had been sent to him. He was more than eager to get his hands on some new projects. The latest project he was trying to fix was an automatic drawer that lifted the cutlery out. It was really hard for some of his friends who were in wheelchairs to be able to see where all the cutlery was in the drawer. While it was true some of the drawers could be lowered, the other option was to put them into a pre-made tray that held forks and spoons, and when they pushed the button on the side, the drawer would come out, and the tray would lift at a forty-five-degree angle, so they would be able to get their own cutlery. Jack had to admit; he thought it was going to be a lot easier than what it had been so far.

He could still recall the times when the tray had lifted, tossing all of the cutlery out all over the floor. However, he found it so satisfying to be able to do this and then give it to someone else to make their lives easier. It brought him a sense of peace, especially when he couldn't find that peace on his own.

"You're in here again working on these projects. You know, if they paid you for the time that you're in here, you could probably retire from that truck," Coram said.

"It's not about the money," Jack replied.

"I know, and I think that's the first problem already."

Jack doesn't even begin to engage in the conversation. Coram might be one of his good friends here, and the both of them may even be truck owners, but that was about where it stopped. Coram didn't understand why he would donate his time without being compensated with the dollar.

"Here, take a look at this," Jack requested.

Coram looked at him work the tray. Jack pushed the button and the drawer eased out and then the tray within the draw slowly lifted to the correct angle and then stopped. Jack was ecstatic.

"Jack, what did you even make this for? Who's going to use it?"

"This was requested, that isn't an issue. In fact, I know a lot of people are going to find this is really useful, and I'm just so happy that I was able to get it done."

Coram went to look at the tray that was standing at forty-five degrees. Jack thought any moment he was going to congratulate him on how good everything looked, but he had forgotten this was Coram.

"I'm not really sure this is going to make sense for whoever you built it for."

Why was he was waiting for the day that Coram would be just as excited?

"Well, they aren't paying you, so I guess it's okay. I mean, the tray isn't the prettiest thing I've ever seen, and the drawer is what it is. Hey, I came by because I saw the college kid by himself. Is he working your truck because he's getting better, or because you needed a break?"

Jack smiled. Coram was dense but not a complete goner.

"I needed some space. Besides I've been thinking the college kid is doing really well. I think that the arrangement of letting him run the truck is going to work for us both. He's made strides, and I think I want to have some more time to do these kind of things. I want to make more things for my group."

Coram looked at the drawer and then at Jack. Jack knew it wasn't going to be a pat on the back and an "I support your decision" comment.

"You know the truck is stable. Make sure the college guy understands that he's being trusted with all of your livelihood."

Jack didn't know why, but he did know that

Coram didn't have the greatest opinion about young people.

"The college student in question is called Lionel, and I think that he'll do a great job."

"I'm not saying that Lionel will do a bad job. Do you remember when you first came here, and you said that you knew how to do some handyman work and you knew how to cook? The first thing I did was offer you a place at my truck just so that you'd be able to get out of the house. You weren't all that thrilled with it, but you know what? You helped me to turn around the income in my truck. If you hadn't done that, you would have gone out there and done some volunteer work for something else and not be able to follow your path and open your own truck."

Coram couldn't seem to accept that it was more important to him after the accident to do things that fulfilled him, rather than to do things that loaded his pocket up. It wasn't that Jack thought money was bad, it was just that he thought money had a place. And it wasn't in the front ruling his whole life.

"I want to thank you, Coram. There were so many things that you suggested that I wouldn't have thought of myself. However, I do still think that there's a time when I need to do the things that make me happy."

"Friend, I'm just concerned that happiness doesn't pay bills. You can help people in the town, but you should keep the sure thing, especially if it's making you money," Coram reminded him.

Jack could have reminded Coram that he hadn't come to the bay penniless. It was true he wasn't as well to do as Reid and the other Chance brothers, but he had enough to live comfortably on. The truck made money, but Jack could live without it if he wanted to. Coram didn't want Jack to stay at home in the garage, so he invited him over to his home with his family.

Jack liked Coram's family. They were very simple and practical. His wife was a good cook and worked in the diner in town. His children were in their teens, and both had part-time jobs in town and were heavily involved in their clubs at school. Coram's family was essentially a greeting card on taking no chances and going the practical way. Jack didn't hold any of that against them. In fact, he was jealous that they were content and happy doing it. What Jack knew was that it just wasn't for him.

Lingering in the back of his mind were Gloria's words. Kathy was with her brother. She was so close, but they had parted on such odd terms that .... Then Jack thought about how they parted. Maybe he had been too sensitive, and she had been right a little bit. He did like working with his hands. He liked talking to people at the truck, but there was something to be said about watching someone use one of his inventions. Jack was going to call Kathy. This supposed argument was silly. Then he heard his phone ping. Someone had sent him a text.

KNOCK, KNOCK, CAN JACK COME OUT TO PLAY?

Jack smiled when he saw Kathy's text.

MAYBE

For a moment, Jack thought of all of those movies he and the guys used to laugh at. The women in the movies would say, "don't seem so eager." He looked at his text and decided all the other items he could add to this text would make him seem so weird. The problem was that Kathy didn't answer back. Jack was waiting, but maybe she needed something else. Just when he was about to write something, he saw the little dots of her responding show up on the bottom of the screen, and he let out a sigh of relief.

MAYBE HE WANTS AN APOLOGY?

Jack sat back and smiled. He didn't want one, but the fact that it was on the table reassured him that this relationship was going to work. Having a partner who was willing to negotiate was a good portent, even if she didn't know it yet.

I'M GOOD BECAUSE YOU WERE RIGHT.

HOLD ON. I'M FRAMING THIS TEXT.

Jack did laugh then. Texting was nice, but he wanted to hear her voice.

"Hello?" she answered tentatively.

"Framing my text? Are you trying to say something?" he asked with a smile in his voice.

"No, of course not, Mr. Man With a Plan, and I'm sure you'll like it."

Jack laughed.

"Does it seem a little high-handed?"

"A bit, but it's not overbearing, so I can let you get away with it for now."

"You know, I read in a women's book that women like that."

"Um-hmm, it was probably written by a man," she replied.

"I'm working on something new in the garage."

"Really?"

"Yes. And while I was working and doing some other things, I did think about what you said."

"Jack, really? I'm sorry. I-I shouldn't have—"

"You shouldn't have what? There'll be times when both of us will say things that need to be said. We may not like it, but the fact is that it needs to be said by somebody."

"Jack—"

"I know you don't know what to say it, but let me start out by saying I think that you are right. I should probably be spending some more time, or at least have a more dedicated schedule to doing the dignity project. I'm thinking the real issue, is I really don't know how to do that."

"Do which part?"

"I guess all of it. I mean, the people that I know in this project are people that I know, not necessarily a business or anything."

"Well, you happen to be in luck."

"Oh, do I?"

"Yes, as it would happen, the Chance family is able to assist you."

"I don't know if I can deal with the whole family. I—"

"No worries, I have you there as well. I will help you out and walk you through this perilous process of setting up the company or foundation, whichever one you prefer, to distribute your products."

"And the price for this service?" Jack asked with suspicion in his voice.

"Ah, well, there is a rumor going about that you are very good at setting up outings. I'm going to be around for a bit. Send me an invite for tomorrow."

"Anyplace special?" he asked.

"No, surprise me."

"Are you sure?"

"Yes, Jack. I'm sure."

After the phone call, Jack hung up and danced around the room like a kid. The only thing on his mind was, *she trusts me*. That night, he dreamed about going to the supermarket to get eggs, and every one of the eggs he opened had double yolks in them.

CHAPTER 12

"*A* therapist, huh?" Kathy asked.

Gloria nodded. A smile took over her face.

"I'm so excited. I think that it'll give me an opportunity to work with Reid, and it'll be a new beginning for us."

"Was there something so wrong with the one you all had?" Kathy asked.

"No, Reid is absolutely amazing. It's just that we spend so much time apart, and I really would like for us to do something that both of us are involved in."

Kathy was a little concerned with the explanation.

"Are you sure that changing into a brand-new career and demanding one is really the only way that the both of you can spend some more time together?"

Gloria stopped. "Do you think that I'm not going to be a good therapist?"

"My first answer to that is I think you would be a

great therapist. I'm a little concerned about some things. One, why do you think that you need to change your career to have more time together? Couples need to make sure that they make time for each other, not that they are stuck with each other and can't avoid each other. I think that's a totally different thing going on. The second thing would be, why is the first thing that comes to your mind that you think you're not going to be a good therapist? Or you're asking me if I think you're going to be a good therapist. Going into therapy really should be about a calling to help other people."

Gloria sat down at the kitchen table and folded her hands.

"You're right, of course. Going into therapy shouldn't be about getting closer to your husband. The truth of the matter is, is that I had always secretly wanted to do therapy, but when I was growing up, it didn't seem to pay the amount of money that I thought I needed to take care of myself and my family. Jack and I have always contributed to the house, especially after our father died, and it was always about what would make the most money. When the money finally isn't an issue, I thought I would go and do it. And the fact that Reid has a therapy branch just seemed like everything was falling into place."

Kathy heard Gloria, and she felt better knowing that this wasn't just something to get more time with Reid. And she and Jack had the same problem. Responsibilities or life had gotten in the way of things they were good at or really wanted to do. Kathy reached out and patted Gloria on the hands.

"As long as you're doing it for the right reasons,

then don't worry about it. It will all work out. Is that why you came over today?"

Gloria brightened and then shook her head.

"Oh no! I came by because an unofficial girl meeting was called," Kathy said with a smile. "I didn't have to invite you because you were already here at Reid's.

A little bit of trepidation set in Kathy's heart. She wasn't sure that she liked crowds, and even though it was getting better, this was an unexpected moment.

"What girls are coming over, and do I know them?"

Gloria waved her concerns off and stood up from the table, and loaded the coffee maker.

"Oh, yes, yes. You know everyone. It's going to be Rose, Traci, and Portia."

"You mean Vincent's Traci?"

"I'm not sure that Traci would appreciate you calling her Vincent's, but yes."

Kathy hadn't had much time with Traci. She wanted to spend a little bit more time with her because she was so grateful to her. Out of all of the brothers, the top two that Kathy worried about the most were Vincent and Quinn. Vincent never trusted anyone, and Quinn didn't seem like she could ever catch a break.

"Hey, hey, hey. I know that look. Reid gets that look when he's about to do something that I may not agree with."

"It's okay. I'm not going to do anything rash. I just really wanted to just meet Traci and have some real time with her, that's all. It takes a special woman to deal with my brother. Well, I shouldn't have to tell you. It takes a special woman to deal with all of my brothers."

Gloria filled the coffee cups and brought them to the table.

"I would think that after that whole debacle of someone trying to steal from Vincent, and Traci finding the culprit, all questions would be put to rest about their relationship. Instead, can you believe there is still some media coverage on it, speculating whether Traci is a gold digger or not? I just don't get people," Gloria said.

Kathy thought about how Traci and Vincent had been tested and endured. She wanted that. It was silly, and it wasn't like she believed in fairy tales, but she wanted to have that experience, when a man would go all out for her hand. It sounded so hokey, but there was something endearing about it too.

"You know, I didn't know that you were having a group meeting today. I think Jack is coming by," Kathy said in a sheepish voice.

"Oh, he told you that he was coming? He is soo efficient," Gloria said.

Jack hadn't said anything about Gloria. Maybe she wasn't even the reason he was coming over. Maybe what was happening here was that Jack was coming over for Gloria, and she was here so he would see her as well.

"Well, what's important is that he told everyone that he's coming, right? So why is he coming to see you?"

Kathy's voice must have changed because Gloria stopped and tapped Kathy's hands. "Jack has been working on something for me for the kids. We have been having some issues with some of the kids who want to get on the horses by themselves. I asked Jack to look at this, and he said he could build something that might be able to help. Originally, he told me he would just leave it here, but I was so excited when I heard him talk about it. I figured I might as well be here when he gets here."

There it was. The confirmation that Kathy would use when Jack got here that his work wasn't just for his friends who had discovered. Jack's discoveries were for anyone who needed to find some dignity in doing everyday tasks.

"Jack showed me an invention or two of his."

"He told you about what he does for his friends? He has never taken me to go and drop off any of his work with his friends, so I'm not really sure how this is all going to work out. Do you think that he's any good at it? I mean, he's my brother, so no matter what, I'm going to like it because he put the effort into it. But I was just wondering," Gloria asked.

Kathy felt all sorts of special. Jack had not shared his love of creating items and gadgets with his sister. The fact that the sister was going to accept it no matter what another reason was just why she loved Gloria. However, she knew that Gloria was about to be amazed today.

"You're going to be pleasantly surprised with what he presents to you today," Kathy said, looking at the sense of relief that came over Gloria's face.

"Well, I certainly hope he is using the garage in that house. You know, when we first got here, I thought he was in there doing all sorts of man things with the car, but once I got ready to go in, he just stopped me at the door. It was so bad. I was thinking about paying his friend Coram to smuggle me inside, who for whatever reason could go in and out whenever he chose, but I couldn't go into this sole sanctum."

"I know Jack is protective of his garage, but I think it's where he puts a lot of his heart," Kathy said.

"I know. I kind of feel bad about that whole endeavor as well."

"Why do you say that?" Kathy asked.

"I feel like several times Jack had the opportunity to get up and leave and see whether or not he could start this company on his own. One of the main reasons my brother never seriously considered leaving Inheritance Bay is because I was here, and I stayed here to give him a normal town to come back to," Gloria said. "The thing is, though, is that when I look back on that time, I don't think that it was Jack who needed to have a place to come back to. I think it was me. Which meant I'm the reason that Jack didn't try to go out on his own earlier. He just would never leave his sister."

"I don't want you to take all of that on yourself. At the end of the day, Jack is a grown man, and he can make his own decisions. Besides, if it's any consolation to you, you're not the only one who's been trying to convince Jack to try this new thing that he really loves to do."

"Really?" Gloria asked curiously as she sat looking at Cathy with rapt attention.

"His best friend Paul has also been trying to get him to do the same thing."

"You met Paul?" Gloria asked.

"Yes," Cathy said hesitantly.

"Add on the talk to Paul on the phone, and to be

honest, I have to tell you I wasn't sure what to expect. He sounded like a happy person, but it definitely didn't sound like somebody who was paralyzed, which is what Jack told me. Every time we got ready to meet Paul, something would come up. And I started to think that maybe Paul just wasn't as paralyzed as I thought, or I don't know. Something would be off because he never seemed to want us to meet Paul."

Kathy thought to herself that she could imagine why. Paul wasn't a shy friend, and he would definitely bring up how talented Jack was. Kathy could see that Jack might not have been ready to be put in the spotlight in front of his friends before, but now maybe he had grown a little confidence in what he did and would be able to present in front of a class or in front of the people who didn't realize that there was an unmet need that needed to be addressed in the community. Just then, before Kathy could go on into any more detail or say anything else, the doorbell rang, and Gloria looked as though she were a child on Christmas Day.

"It's Jack. I'll get it."

Kathy was glad that Gloria sprinted to the door because she wasn't sure if she could have gotten up. Her heart was still on the last time they had been together, and they had both said things that she wished she could take back. It was true that it all seemed like it was better on the phone, but this was the moment of truth. When Kathy heard his voice, it was all better.

"Gloria, what are you doing here?"

Kathy smiled. So at least, she knew he expected it to be just them.

"Stop stalling, Jack, and bring it in," Gloria said, looking over his shoulder like a kid on Christmas.

Before he left, he turned and looked at Kathy. "Hi, Kathy."

"Hi, Jack," Cathy replied. With just a few words, she was automatically taken back to being a teenager, holding her breath on the phone as she breathed on the phone and hoped he knew they were communing on a different level.

"Oh, my goodness, the both of you. I just can't stand it. Give me my stool first, and then the both of you can do whatever. I just stare at each other's eyes and breathe," Gloria teased.

Jack nodded and then went outside, and a few moments later, he came back in. He seemed to have something that looked like nothing more than a wooden stoop. When he put it down, he turned it toward them.

"Okay, this is how it works. As you can see, it looks just like a standard stoop. However, there is an indentation here where you can put your foot in it. When you do that, it releases the four wheels so that you can move it left or right or anywhere that you need to."

"My goodness, I hadn't even thought about them having to move it. Jack, you're really good at this kind of thing."

Kathy could see Jack start to blush. However, she was more familiar with Jack's attention to detail and knew the show wasn't over yet.

"Wait, Gloria. I have to explain the whole thing."

"There's more?" Gloria asked.

"Yes. So, this is how it works. If you push once, it brings the wheels up. If you push in the slide the second time, it locks it down in place so that you can use it to step up on it. On the side, you'll notice that there is a little handle. You can always use your foot and push on the handle, and what it does is elevate the stoop up. So if you are a little shorter than the average person, maybe you need to go up another six inches and then lock it in place, so then you can go ahead and mount the horse."

"Reid is going to be so thrilled. This was just what we were looking for, trying to find a way to balance things out so that some of the kids could mount the horse on their own. Jack, you are really amazing, and I'm so sorry that I didn't really give this enough credit when I saw it before."

"You could only make it as much of a priority as I did. Being with you is the priority."

Just like that, it was a gut punch to Kathy. If being with Gloria was the priority, then why flirt? Kathy didn't mind visiting Inheritance Bay, but she didn't want to live here. She wanted to live upstate in her comfort zone and in a place that allowed her to think. Then as if he hadn't been talking to Gloria, he turned to Kathy.

"Are you ready to hit the road?"

Kathy smiled, and then remembered that Gloria was having a girls' meet-up. Kathy turned toward Gloria, and Gloria waved her off.

"After the amazing work that he's done, there's no way I could take you away from his plan today. I'll make sure to update you on whatever comes up, and I have to say to you both that I hope you have the best time ever."

Kathy turned toward Jack and gave him a wide smile. "You know, Gloria, I'm hoping that we have a great time as well, but for me to figure out if it's going to be a great time, it would probably help if I knew what we were doing or where we were going," Kathy said.

Jack smiled at her and then reached into a nearby closet and pulled out a light jacket. "If that's going to be your best pitch for the day, you're not going to be able to get a whole lot of information."

"You know I'm not particularly fond of surprises, right?" Kathy said as she put her arm into her jacket that Jack held open for her.

"Too much predictability in a person's life can kill creativity. I can assure you, lots of people want to make sure that your creativity keeps going."

"And the place that we're going to go is going to help my creativity somehow?" Kathy asked, hoping to be able to tease out some clues about where they were actually going.

"To admit that is a better try at getting the information."

"Why does it have to be a surprise? Why can't you just tell me?" Kathy asked. They were interrupted by Gloria laughing.

"You know, when I look at you two, I'm not even sure which one of you I want to root for. But both of you are just so cute," Gloria said. "I will leave the two of you two this then."

After Gloria had left the room, Kathy turned to face Jack and put her hands on her hips.

"Why don't you just tell me where we're going? What's the big deal?"

Jack looked at her and then smiled. "It's not a big deal. It's just a matter of trust. If you really don't feel as though you can trust me, then I'll tell you. Because no matter what, I don't want you to be uncomfortable."

Kathy couldn't believe he had said that. Just a matter of trust. Did he say just? Were they at the place where she could trust him?

"Kathy?"

Kathy mumbled and then zipped up her jacket.

"They better have good food where we're going. That's all I have to say on the matter."

So, with eyes wide open, Kathy walked out the door, hand in hand with Jack.

CHAPTER 13

"*T*he soup was amazing. It only goes to confirm that you rock at it."

Kathy smiled at Jack. Jack knew in his heart that she had no idea what her words meant to him.

"From a person who sees new business ideas come and go all the time, I want you to know I take that as high praise," Jack said.

"I don't have amnesia, Jack. I also know that you were the one who said you weren't interested in maybe doing more with your talent."

Jack sighed. Of course, she would remember that. He had used it as a lure to bring her outside, but now he wasn't so sure it was a good idea. That was the only reason he had said it. Making things and giving people their independence and confidence was something that was so near and dear to his heart, but he had been afraid to trust that he could do it consistently.

Jack opened the door and showed her inside. He

couldn't wait to get to the other side of the truck and to get them to their final destination.

"Jack, I think I showed a lot of trust by getting in the car. Why don't you just tell me where we're going now?"

Jack laughed out loud and started up the truck. "Wow, you weren't kidding when you said that you don't have any patience at all."

"Why don't you try to think of something else while we go along our way?"

"What could possibly be more important than where we're going right now?"

Jack pointed out of the side window, and Kathy followed it to see Gloria standing at the window, waving hysterically.

"Now, I personally think that it's funny that my sister is standing out the door wishing us a good time."

"Maybe I should have asked her," Kathy moaned.

"Maybe," Jack said with a chuckle. As the truck pulled out and they stopped at their first light, Jack decided to give her a hint.

"We are going to be in this car for about two hours. We should get to know each other."

"Two hours, you say? If we travel that far, it will either put us in a city or the woods."

"We are not going to the city," Jack confirmed.

"Well, which one—"

"That was all the hint you are getting, so let's move on. You know all there is to know about me, but I know very little about you."

"Me? There isn't much to know. I had a mother. She gave me up. I was in the foster care system, my brother found me, and now you've kidnapped me."

Jack laughed.

"Okay, so we know you are a bit dramatic."

"Dramatic!" Kathy scoffed.

"Okay, the jump was a bit extra," Jack laughed. "I want to know about the woman after foster care. We all have things that shape us, but what matters is what we do after that."

Kathy didn't say anything, and for a little while, he thought she was going to ignore him totally.

"Well, there isn't all that much to tell. What I can tell you is that what I learned going from foster home to foster home is that you didn't get kept unless you could do something amazing. It was always the way of things that the people who knew how to do something or who were very good at school, or someone who just made the foster parents look better, had a better chance of getting adopted."

Jack heard the words, and his heart bled for her. It was true that he, his sister, and his mom did not always get along, but it was never an issue about her not being there or him ever doubting that she cared about them all equally.

"So, what does that mean exactly?" Jack asked.

"What it means is that I didn't have a skill set that anybody could see, so my obvious value wasn't there."

He gripped the wheel and tried not to cringe as he heard Kathy say something that he thought was so horrible, as a matter of fact. He shouldn't have been surprised because that was part of the reason they had had an argument. She had seen what he could do with his hands and what he did to his friends in order to restore some of their dignity, and she had tangible value. She didn't think that she had any particular value because she didn't build anything, but she was wrong.

"I happen to think you are amazing and bring so much value to those around you. We won't even mention all the people you helped start new businesses or the services those business serve to the community of Inheritance Bay."

"Maybe. But I think any of my brothers could do it," Kathy said nonchalantly.

"I think if making money was that easy, a lot of people would be doing it," Jack joked. Jack stopped the car and picked up some road snacks at the service station. When they got back into the car, Kathy couldn't resist teasing him.

"You have enough chips in here to have your own dipping contest."

"I don't want to faint from hunger," Jack defended as he popped a chip in his mouth.

Kathy laughed. "We are an hour out. I think you would need some more time to faint."

"Okay, you may be right, but I'd rather be safe."

Once again, that comfortable silence fell between them. Jack loved that they didn't have to talk all the time. In the past, when he wasn't talking, it was a huge problem for his past relationships, so this was a pleasant surprise.

"Jack, can I ask you a question?"

He preened on the inside. If she felt comfortable enough to open up and share, then then the trip was bringing them closer together.

"You can ask me any question that you want."

"You are obviously very passionate about making

things for other people so that they can keep their dignity even to be more mobile. Why is it when I pointed out that it's such a good thing and it's so valuable that you were so angry?"

For once, Jack was happy that he was driving, and they weren't looking directly at one another. It was so hard to explain, but he owed it to Kathy to find a way.

"I wasn't angry, even though I could see how it might have looked that way. It was a hard thing for me to try to figure out what I wanted to do after I was able to walk again. I want you to know that when you can't walk, people who you thought were friends don't stay. You find out who's your real family. More importantly, I think you get to find out what people really thought about you before the accident. If I were honest, I would tell you I had different thoughts about myself before and after that accident. Even with all of that going on, I have to say I still wanted to hold on to something that was a part of the old me. I wasn't ready to completely let go of the person who wanted to do something in cooking."

"And does it have to be one or the other?" Kathy asked.

"Maybe it's not about me choosing, but it's about me not failing. You know, in the restaurant business, we see lots of people who come in with recipes from their family and the hopes and dreams they've nurtured from childhood. Unfortunately, none of those mean anything in business. Business requires that you are able to look at everything objectively and find out what you can make at a profit and for how long because it's not just you. Other families are depending on you as well. I didn't know how I was going to be able to do that. How would I be able to pick one invention over the other or one project over the other? How do I pick which one is more worthy? So I made it into a hobby and kept it safe. The day you asked me about it, I was frustrated, but the frustration wasn't from you. It was a frustration that I had been holding on to. You just happened to let it out."

"Well, I'm glad we got that out of the way."

"Excuse me? Kathy, did you just hear what I said?"

"I did hear what you said. I think you need to think about where you are now and not where you used to be. According to all of the papers, I have the Magic touch when it comes to making businesses. According to all of your friends, you have the magic touch when it comes to making inventions. It's not a matter of making choices of what to do and what not to do. Those things will go away when you have money at your fingertips.," Cathy said.

Jack was thinking long and hard as he pulled up to the trail site. He turned to look at her with a wide smile only to see her furrowed brow as she looked out of the window.

"I know this place," Kathy murmured.

Jack parked the car and then tapped her on her knee to get her attention.

"I think you're right. The two of us working as a team should be able to solve any problem we run into."

"This is the retreat run by Dr. Talls," Kathy murmured.

"Dr. Talls? I don't know her, but I do know a

woman named Yesenia Troykin," Jack said and waited to see if the name rang a bell with Kathy.

It took a moment, but then Kathy's eyes lit up with recognition.

"I know Yesenia. She was the first woman we brought here. She needed to relocate. She and her son came here to the camp while she learned the skills she needed to work in computers, I believe. She and her son now live in Inheritance Bay, if I remember correctly."

Jack nodded.

"Yesenia and her son come to the truck every Friday. She is the director of Application Support at the elementary school. I was sitting and talking to her when she told me her story. What was the most important part was that she said she would have never been able to turn her life around if it hadn't been for this place. It's my understanding that this place as a concept was passed over several times. It was only when a group of doctors approached you that you decided to give it a go and fund them," Jack said.

Kathy nodded.

"Dr. Talls wasn't running it then, but it was a great idea, and I could see how it would be beneficial to the people who needed the service and to the land. This park wasn't generating enough income to keep it clean and watch the health of the animals."

Jack leaned over and put his forehead against hers.

"You see, you bring value to things that everyone can see and benefit from. Now let's go. I hear today is an open barbecue day, and I wanted to try some new cuisine that I hear rivals my truck."

Kathy looked him in the eye and smiled.

"So, we're here to check out the competition?"

Jack smiled.

"I'm trying to impress an investor. I want her to know I can multitask and keep business focused."

"I hear you're doing a good job, but we'll have to check back in later to see the final marks."

"Really?"

"Really, You're going to have to work for it, Jack."

Jack leaned in and placed his lips over hers, and then pulled back.

"It's not a problem. You're so worth it. Now let's go and stop distracting me."

CHAPTER 14

"*P*lease tell me we are not eating there."

Kathy looked at the blanket that was laid out on the grass. In the middle of the blanket, there was a picnic basket, and there were two plates, and two cups already set out for them. As far as she was concerned, there couldn't have been a worse place to put the setup. There was no way to hide from anyone sitting on this blanket.

"I could tell you that we're not going to eat there, but I think that when we didn't move, it would become very apparent to you that we were. Is this really a problem?" Jack asks.

Kathy wanted to yell back at him, "No, it's not a problem. It's a catastrophe."

"I don't like being in the middle of nowhere. You don't really like being in the center of attention."

"Look around, Kathy. I'm not saying that there aren't other people here, but they're not all here to see you. I want you to be able to claim back some of your own independence about where you go," Jack said.

Kathy looked around the area, and truth be told, this wasn't such a bad place to be. Besides, she had been here before when she came to do the setup all those many years ago.

"Fine, fine. Let's just sit, and we'll get through this," Kathy said.

"I like that we're going to go for the Winston Churchill move that just says keep going until you get to the end."

"You are a terrible pep coach."

"It's true; it's not my specialty. What are my specialties? To be able to tell you the truth. I'm here with you, and no one and nothing is going to surprise you or shock you. I won't leave you here. And if it should rain, I'm even going to be manly enough to give you my jacket to put over your head."

Kathy rolled her eyes. "Well, I guess chivalry isn't completely dead," she said sarcastically.

"To make sure I keep to my word, and I don't leave you or your shadow, not even for a moment, I had the basket brought down here."

Kathy smiled and then looked at the basket.

"You can prove to me that chivalry isn't dead by serving up the food. Or are you going to let me just starve right here?"

"Wow, I can tell somebody is hangry," Jack said with a smile.

Over the next hour, Jack went out of his way to be the perfect host. Every so often, someone would walk by and maybe linger for a minute or two, but never longer than that. With the fresh, clean air and the cleared-out areas for the picnic, it was the perfect day.

"So, we're out here. I've laid the food out to appease you. This isn't so bad, is it?"

Kathy looked around, and if she were honest, the answer would be no.

"I know my hesitation to be outside can be a problem," Kathy said.

"It's not a problem. I just need to understand it, that's all," Jack said.

"It all started with me being in different homes and being the smallest person in the group. Some homes are very nice, and I was never in one of those. I usually got picked up by someone who thought I was going to be able to be a good worker or to be able to run errands. It turned out I was sickly as a child, and so I would be in places, and parents would come up to me and just tap me on the shoulder, scaring me. I got tired of people sneaking up on me, and so I learned how to stick closer to the walls. Then when I finally got old enough, before Reid found me, I was in a relationship that wasn't very healthy."

"If this is painful for you, we don't have to go over it. I just wanted to make sure that I understood what the boundaries were, and I wanted to make sure I was respecting your wishes."

"Jack, you are definitely the one who's always respecting my wishes. Sometimes I wish I knew what I really wanted as much as you want to give it to me. At any rate, I was also in a relationship that taught me to make myself small. People are less noticeable on the side or against the wall. There was a time that

I would be out in the open and hope that it would all end. Then one day, I went to school, and I was able to help someone else out. It was silly because it was a math problem. I decided then that I could be useful and began, from that day on, to make a plan of escape. I didn't have to worry about that because Reid showed up, and I've been safe ever since."

Jack reached across and grabbed her hand. It was the simple things that he did that brought tears to her eyes.

"You are so sentimental, Jack."

"Maybe, but I'd rather give too much and make sure you're okay Kathy," he said. "I'd like to make sure you don't worry about if you are in the center or the middle of the room. I'll be there no matter what."

Kathy looked at their joined hands on the blanket. She wanted to stay like this forever and feel safe. Dr. Talls had told her that this time would come, and she would feel safe with another person besides Reid. Dr. Talls had also said they needed to work on some other issues. Kathy had decided that it wasn't really worth it. Reid was happy, and that was all that mattered at the time, but now that she was with Jack, there was that twinge of hope for something more.

Kathy could still feel the passersby take an extra look at her and Jack. When she was with him, it didn't seem so bad. Kathy let out a deep breath and tried to just concentrate on the moment she was in. If Jack saw something in her, then maybe she could find out what it was. Kathy wanted to tell him that this picnic had made up her mind that she was going to try to go to a small conference in New York City. It was a day event, but Kathy was sure she could do it, and when she did, she'd be a whole person for Jack. She didn't want their lives to be in small, hidden places on retreats because of her, that was, if they were going to have anything together. She wanted to be a whole person for the person she cared about.

Jack looked in the basket and then back at Kathy.

"I forgot the dessert. When the basket was packed, I must have left it out, or I don't know," he said, clearly frustrated.

"It's not really that big of a deal," Kathy said.

"Would you mind if I went back up the road and got us some desserts from the main house?"

There must have been some show of hesitation on Kathy's face when Jack said that because he reached out to put a hand over hers. "Hey, it's no problem. Maybe we don't need dessert."

Instantly, Kathy felt horrible. It was just to the main house. How long would he actually be gone? She could surely make it on her own on a blanket. This was what she hated. He was going to do something every other guy would do for a woman, and here she was, wondering about being in the open and looking around to see where people could be hiding.

"Go ahead. Make sure you get something good," Kathy said with a smile on her face. It was a shame that it wasn't as authentic as she wanted it to be. Kathy decided to lie down after Jack left. She didn't realize how relaxing the outdoors could be. Then she felt a hand on her shoulder. At first, she tensed, but then she opened her eyes and saw Jack. Her body relaxed, and she saw that Jack was looking at her with a raised eyebrow.

"What is it? Is there a bug on me?" Kathy asked, trying not to panic in case he said yes.

"No, it's just that I didn't realize that you would just drift off and forget about me. Here I thought I would have an eagerly awaiting woman for dessert, and I find she has decided to take a cat nap, forgetting her gallant knight who fearlessly ventured down the path and—"

"Okay, I get it. I wasn't waiting breathlessly for you to return. I'm so sorry," Kathy said. Seeing him asking for the compliment but at the same time being that playful friend was something that endeared him to her like nothing else. "Forgive me. I was just resting up to be able to appreciate the bounty you were bringing back."

"Ah, that is more appropriate. I will share my bounty with you," he said loftily. He had a platter and pulled it back, and on it was an assortment of donuts, cake, and cookies.

"I see you foraged well," she said with as much seriousness as she could get into her voice.

"Yes, you may go forth and eat now. I feel sufficiently appreciated."

Kathy found herself giggling at his antics and then proceeded to eat. After a few moments, both of them had consumed at least one cookie and one donut. Kathy looked at Jack and gave him a wide smile.

"And what have I done to earn the sunshine that you are bestowing upon me?"

"I didn't think I would, but I do like it here. I like being outside."

"Ah, I tell you. I knew that you would love it as soon as you were able to be in this fresh air. Of course, it doesn't hurt to have pastries as well. That smooths everything over. The only thing left is for us to relax in the sun." Jack got up and walked to the other side of the blanket until he was sitting behind Kathy. "Lean back. I've got you."

Kathy closed her eyes and enjoyed the moment. She would have never thought that this would have been possible to be outside leaning against an attractive man in the middle of a park. She felt no fear and no trepidation.

"This really isn't so bad. I thought today was going to be an absolute horror when I saw this park, but I have to say, you made it into a dream."

"Okay, we are not going to let you be the girl to give the inspirational speech on good deeds. But I thank you anyway. Just to be able to get you to come outside and for us to have a good time, it was all worth it. Although I don't know if my ego will ever recover from sleep being more important than pastries, but at least you woke up."

Kathy turned to look at him, and their gazes connected. The laughing fell away, and at that moment, she could have fallen into his gaze forever. Then it was like slow motion when his hand came up and brushed an errant curl back from her face.

He leaned closer to her, and just before his lips touched hers, he whispered, "Just so that you know, you've made my day too." When Jack pressed his lips against hers, it wasn't demanding or rushed. It was perfect. It was then that Kathy knew she was going to the event. She'd get better for Jack. This would not be a onetime event. She could do this on her own without Dr. Talls or anyone else. She could make herself whole.

CHAPTER 15

*J*ack looked at the toilet paper roll down the track and then smiled.

The track was securely inside of the bathroom cabinet, and when the toilet paper rolled down, it fit perfectly into the holder. Jack could make the track longer if he needed to. The phone rang. Jack wasn't expecting anyone, so he jumped when he heard his phone, hitting his head inside the cabinet.

"Hello?!"

"Wow, you are so grumpy. I'll call later," Kathy said.

"No! I'm sorry. I just banged my head."

"I'm sorry. I didn't mean to interrupt. It's early afternoon. I thought you'd be in the park. If you need to leave, I can—"

"Kathy, stop trying to get off the phone. This is the best part of my day."

"Well, I just called to say thank you. I had a great time yesterday."

Jack smiled as he took a seat on the floor, rubbing

his head. "I knew you would, but it's nice of you to admit it too," Jack said.

"Okay, so much for being humble today. I've got work to do."

"Ah, yes. You have dreams to fulfill. I will go to my truck today and work in my garage until you return. Trying to find meaning without you near me."

"You're too much. I'll see you when I get back. Paperwork needs me."

Jack hung up, and there wasn't any mention of deep feelings or the kiss, but he had to be patient. Kathy was worth the wait and effort. Jack wiped his hands on his pants and then got up. Kathy was right. He should be going to the park to help the new kid out. The kids were out of school on recess holiday, and they could be a beast.

Just when he was about to cover his latest creation, there was a knock on the garage door. The door opened.

"Jack? Are you in this fire trap?"

Jack sighed and wondered what he'd done to deserve seeing Reid now. "Yes, I'm here, but it will get you first. I'm closer to a fire extinguisher and an exit."

"Ha, ha. I'm not worried. You have to save me, so Kathy isn't upset," he said as he came around the corner. The truth of it was that he was right, but Jack wasn't in the mood to tell him.

"What brings you down here?" Jack asked.

Jack noticed that Reid was touching everything. He wanted to tell him to keep his hands to himself, but he thought of Kathy and breathed through it.

"The guys are getting together for dinner, and I'm inviting you."

Jack was taken aback.

"What?"

"Yeah, don't look so shocked. Grayson actually wanted us to meet, and you're one of us now, so you can come too. Quinn backed out, saying he had work, so we had a spot to fill anyway."

Jack smiled to himself. He thought about making Reid squirm, but it wasn't in him.

"I'll be there. Text me the address."

"Great, we'll see you there then."

Jack watched Reid as he walked slowly out, eyeing every item in the garage. He wasn't sure what the dinner was about, but he was glad that Reid had left his inner sanctum. Now he would go back to making the cabinet larger to hold more toilet paper and think about the dinner when it was time to go.

It was seven thirty, and Jack found himself sitting at the table with the Chance brothers, Grayson, Reid, Vincent, and himself. What was worse was none of them seemed to be happy. The waitress had dropped off the fries and given everyone a soda. Someone had to break the silence.

"Rose is pregnant," Grayson blurted out. The other men at the table were silent. Jack looked at Grayson.

"Congratulations!" Jack said.

Reid and Vincent shook their heads and said in unison, "He doesn't know any better."

Jack looked around the table.

"What am I missing?"

"Listen, I just got the hang of the twins. I'm not even sure that I'm doing that right. Now she's pregnant again. It's just another opportunity for me to mess up with someone innocent," Grayson said as his head fell into his hands.

"Why don't you tell her?" Jack asked.

Reid looked at Jack and shook his head. "Dude, you better get smarter if you are going into a relationship with Kathy," Reid said. "You can share if you want, but then there will be a whole lot of sharing and you have to ask yourself if you are ready for that."

"Like what? I tell Kathy everything," Jack replied, lost.

"My goodness, everything?" Vincent said, horrified.

"Yes, why not? I love her," Jack said.

"Well, I love Traci too, but we don't share everything. In fact, sometimes I have to wait for her to share. Like I'm waiting for her to tell me that she wants another kid and she's been going to the fertility clinic," Vincent said glumly.

Jack was confused.

"Is it that you don't want kids?"

Vincent stretched his neck and took a deep breath before letting his shoulders fall visibly.

"I don't think it's that I don't want kids. It's just I don't come from great stock. So, me having a kid, what am I going to teach a kid? How to hire a private investigator and how not to trust? Nah, I think I need more time, so I don't mess the kid up," Vincent said.

Jack looked at the men at the table and thought that not even a couple of weeks ago, he thought he wasn't in the same league with these guys. He was worried that he was just a food truck guy, and they were all big-wheeling rich guys, but to hear them talk, they were in a worse place than he could ever be. Then he turned to Reid.

"So, is Gloria pregnant too?" Jack asked with a smile in his voice.

"No, but I think I wish she were. She's decided to become a therapist and help me with the therapy ranch," Reid said glumly.

"She told me. I thought you would be thrilled," Jack said.

Reid rubbed his neck and then took some fries from the table.

"You see, Jack, the problem isn't that I don't want to spend more time with her. The issue is that Gloria is a powerhouse of the organization. She's already telling me how she wants to change everything. You know what? She may even be right about the changes and that we need them," Reid finished off.

"So, the issue is…." Jack prompted.

"The issue is that this is my dream and my relaxing place. I love Gloria, but I like it the way it is. Not some well-oiled machine."

Jack looked at them all and was interrupted by the waitress, who brought more bread to the table. The men dove in and went to work on the bread. When it was gone, Jack looked at them all and then put his napkin on the table.

"What's wrong?" Reid asked Jack.

"Gentlemen. I have a cabinet to finish, and I think you all just need to comfort each other so you can talk to your better halves. I appreciate the invite, but I realize Kathy, and I don't have this problem."

"It must be so because she's going to New York

to the day conference by herself to show she's in a good place to have a relationship."

"What?" Jack said, looking at Reid

"So much for sharing everything," Vincent muttered.

"Yeah, I thought you knew She stopped seeing her doctor and was sure she could beat her phobia so she could be better," Reid said.

"No, I didn't know because I would have told her not to."

"Not to," Reid echoed. "This is the first time she's wanted to go out in the open by herself. Why would you want to sabotage her getting better?" Reid asked heatedly.

"The issue is there is nothing wrong with Kathy as is," Jack said.

"We know that" Grayson said in a calm voice.

"Oh, please. Let's not pretend. She can't go out in public, and that is a problem. If she's trying to get a normal life, why are you against it?" Reid argued.

"I'm arguing because if she does or doesn't, she's fine with me. If she wants to do this because it's a goal, fine, but she shouldn't do this because she thinks she's less or not normal."

"I don't think it matters why she does it at all," Reid argued. "She's doing it, and when it works, she'll feel better," Reid stated with his hands crossed over his chest. Jack stood up and went to stand behind Reid where he leaned down and whispered in his ear.

"The sooner she does this, will she feel better or will you?" After that, Jack walked out of the restaurant. They didn't understand. He loved Kathy as is. Phobia and all.

CHAPTER 16

"*W*here did all of these people come from?" Kathy murmured as she stood at the check-in desk. She hadn't talked to anyone, and she was already feeling like there were too many people who had brushed against her and men who just seemed to show up in front of her, smiling in greeting.

It turned out this was a one-day venture capital party, and she had been identified as an angel, someone who has money to invest. Kathy was thinking that she didn't need the name tag with wings. She was sure a lot of people would know her by name and wasn't that really the only time she wanted someone to talk to her?

The young lady at the hotel front desk gave Kathy a huge welcoming smile.

"They aren't even all here. A lot of the conference will show up for the dinner and ball tonight, where a lot of the one-on-one talking will happen."

One-on-one talking? Kathy wanted to ask the young lady to explain that a little further.

"Is there anywhere quiet where I could regroup myself?"

The girl gave her an odd look and then quickly looked beyond her before tapping on her computer.

"We have a conference that just left, so the second floor of the hotel may have some quiet spots. You do know that you can reserve a room if you'd like on this floor if you want to have meetings in a quiet place," the woman offered.

Kathy wanted to reach across and hug the woman.

"I'd love to schedule two of those if you could?"

The young lady's eyes lit up, and she set arranged it. After giving Kathy all of the information, Kathy made a beeline to one of her reserved rooms. She took a seat and pulled out her phone and considered calling Jack.

Kathy had deliberately not told Jack. She could just imagine trying to explain to Jack that she had to try and do this conference so that she would be a whole woman for him. Kathy imagined saying a whole woman for him and seeing Jack look at her as if she had lost her mind. Jack would say she didn't need to be here. He would say that she was fine just the way she was. The problem was that Kathy wanted to do everything to make sure they had the best start in the relationship.

The temptation to reach out to him was so hard. Kath walked to the window and looked outside, and all she could see was all those people everywhere. What happened if she had a panic attack and then fell apart and lost all the ground that she'd made? It was so funny how two people could have one goal and decide to go about it in such different ways. Kathy wanted Jack to agree with her and support her in this move.

Then a knock on the door broke her out of her reverie. It was probably someone in the wrong place. Already, Kathy was starting to stress as she opened the door to send them away.

"Hey, little sister," Reid said. "I can see you already found a nice hidey hole."

Kathy jumped into his arms and pulled him into the room and closed the door.

"Why are you here?"

"I'm here because this is a big step for you, and I wanted to be here, silly."

Kathy looked at Reid and realized that she was glad he was there, but she wanted someone else to be there as well.

"It was easy to find you, Kathy. I mean, when it comes to giving money, some people know your face better than they know your name, which is kind of funny when you consider it all," Reid said. "I was hoping to come in with you in case you felt the crowd was a bit much. I think it probably is."

"No, part of me coming was to walk in on my own, and I was fine," Kathy lied. She would have paid good money for someone to walk into the conference with her. The problem was, the person she would have paid she hadn't told.

"I knew if you just put yourself out there, you would be able to do this. You have the most amazing resolve that I've seen in another person."

"So your thought is that my will alone will change me?"

Reid ran his hands through his hair and then paced for a moment.

"Look, I'm not trying to change you. I want to be here to support you. Are you feeling good and strong?"

Kathy wasn't sure what she was feeling. This was feeling more and more like she needed Jack to be here as well. It was true that she had read all of the self-help books. She had listened to the rah-rah squad of Reid. It was just within her reach. She would be on the path of becoming ..... normal?

"Hey, no matter what, I want you to know that I'm so proud that you decided to try this."

Kathy plastered a smile on her face and nodded. Another knock on the door made her jump, but Reid reached out to her.

"I saw a couple of people and told them to come here so I can do some business. Do you mind?"

Kathy nodded and then pointed to the other door. She hadn't thought she'd need the room to escape to, but it was just another sign that she needed some more time. She just hoped that whatever she needed, it would be done by the end of the day.

The drive to New York was just as unpleasant as Jack thought it would be. Jack had debated if he should even come to the city. It wasn't like Kathy had invited him. He was still so angry that she hadn't even thought to tell him. All of those concerns were put behind him when he considered how she might be in trouble during this event. He wasn't prepared for her to be ready to be in a crowd this big. Regardless of the outcome, he personally felt he was going to be there, just in case she needed anything.

Registering for the one-day conference hadn't been an issue at all. He hoped that Kathy didn't look at the people looking for funding. Jack had put his truck as a possible investment, and he had received a couple of people who actually wanted to invest in it. They said they at least would be willing to talk to him at today's conference. All of those possibilities were put behind him as he thought about what Kathy must be going through being in the midst of all of these people. New York was a beautiful place to visit, but it definitely wasn't a place to visit if you had a problem with crowds.

Jack walked into the hotel, and automatically, the noise was cut off, and the air conditioner engulfed him in a welcoming embrace. Jack saw the signs for the conference and walked up to the second floor to see how many people had actually arrived. It was just like he thought it was going to be. It was a crush. He went to the front desk so that he could sign in. After the front desk girl gave him his name tag, she also gave him a message.

"It seems as though a Mr. Chance will be waiting for you for lunch. He's already arranged a private setting, and if you get there early, he said to give him a call, and he would make sure to come down."

Maybe he had taken his concerns to heart. Or was it that Jack was more transparent than he knew? At any rate, he texted Reid to let him know that he was going to be in the room. Jack found the lunch area fairly quickly, and five to ten minutes later, Reed showed up with all smiles.

"Can you believe that she's here?" Reid said as he took a seat.

"No, I can't," Jack said, looking around the place.

"I have to say, I wasn't sure if we were going to get along, but if you can inspire Kathy like this, I'm willing to give you a second chance."

"I think that second chance you're talking about isn't really a second chance. I mean, it was clear that you thought no one would ever be worthy to touch Kathy's shoes, much less go out with her."

Reid shrugged. "Kathy is special, delicate, and rich. It tends to bring out the worst in people."

Jack knew his lack of money was an issue for Reid, but it wasn't an issue for Kathy or him, so he didn't really see why anyone else was concerned. When Jack heard Kathy's brother talk about her, he made it seem as though she were completely helpless. Jack didn't understand how her brother could look at her and not see the strong and wonderful woman that she was. Kathy was like everyone else, having some flaws and some challenges that she had to work through daily, but he had never met a more exciting, intelligent woman.

Jack's hands were folded, and his thumbs were fidgeting as he looked around the room. Even in this private room, Jack could see the bodies outside in the hallway.

"Calm down," Reid said. "You don't have to defend her here."

Jack looked around the place again and then focused on Reid.

"I disagree. I think this is just the kind of place she needs defense against."

"Jack, you are suffocating her. She can do this."

"That's the problem here, Reid. You don't know that she can do this or that she's ready."

"She talks to these people all the time. Kathy manages a lot of the money in this room already. They won't do anything that will endanger their money. If they have anything negative to say, they will keep it to themselves and—"

"Reid, she deals with these people on Zoom, chats, and phone calls. You are hoping they will contain themselves because of money. How long do you think it will be before she notices that there is something wrong? Then the world she is comfortable in will be gone. Is this coming out worth possibly taking away the world she knows?" Jack asked.

"Let's not argue over how this is going. Why don't we just go see Kathy?"

Jack held up his hand. "She doesn't know I'm here. Let's use our heads for once," Jack said. He picked up his phone and called the front desk.

"Hello?"

"Hello, I'm at the VC conference. My name is Jack Danvers, and I wanted to know if there were appointment slots for Kathy Chance?"

"Hold, please."

Reid gave Jack a thumbs up, and Jack shook his head and waited.

"Hello?"

"Yes?"

"Yes, Ms. Chance has several spots open we can schedule you for. The only update she has in her schedule is that all of her appointments will be via Zoom. Is that okay?"

Hearing the words, Reid deflated, and Jack let out a sigh.

"No, it's fine. I'll see if I can see her at the luncheon or dinner," Jack said.

"Oh, Ms. Chance will not be attending. She's ordered her food to her meeting room."

"Ah, thank you," Jack said and then hung up. "So, I'm curious. What do you think now?"

Reid stood up and paced back and forth. "You know, maybe this wasn't the conference for her to start in. Maybe Kathy needs to go someplace that's not in New York, and she can ease into it there."

"You have got to be kidding me, right?" Jack looked at Kathy's brother, and he couldn't believe what he was seeing. "This isn't worth it."

"How do you know?" Reid fired back. "How do you know?"

"You need to let your guilt go, so it doesn't push Kathy to do things that she's not ready for."

"I'm doing what's best for her, so she can..."

"You found her when you did, and you can't change that. Everyone, especially Kathy is grateful that you found her and gave her an amazing life," Jack said.

"Maybe, but it wasn't soon enough, and now she's crippled—"

Jack struck first and didn't even let Reid finish. Reid looked up at Jack, scrambling to return the blow.

Jack held his hands up. "I'm sorry. If you want to take a shot at me, go right ahead. But there was no way I was going to let you say that there is anything wrong with Kathy. I know that she is not what everyone else is, and that's not a crime. She is amazing, full of life, smart, and funny. I'm so fortunate to have found her, and I'm so happy that she sees something in me. The one thing I will not allow, not even from her brother, is for someone to say that just because she is having a challenge, she is somehow less than anyone else. Kathy will find her way and her confidence, but everyone around her has to stop giving her rules about how she's supposed to do it and when she's supposed to do it. She made a big statement that she was going to do this on her own without the doctor as if working with a doctor is a problem.

"You all say that you love her. Then you all need to treat her as if right now and today; if she does nothing else and nothing changes, you'll still love her. Love shouldn't be conditional."

Jack looked at Reed, standing up, holding his nose. Jack walked out and went to find out where Kathy's rooms were so he could sit outside of them in case she needed anything.

CHAPTER 17

*T*raci walked into the house lit by candlelight. This was worse than she thought.

"Vincent?" she called out tremulously.

Traci followed the candle trail, and it led her to the dining room table, where Vincent sat at the head, waiting for her.

"Hey, gorgeous. I'm glad you came over. It would have been pretty bad to have all this set up, and the woman of the hour wasn't present."

Traci had a brown envelope under her arm and placed it in a chair, and then went to Vincent.

"Thank you for this. I've been having a day," Traci said.

"That is what the word is around town," Vincent said into her hair. When they pulled apart, Traci sat in a chair on his right, and he didn't let her hand go on the table.

"Vincent?" Traci asked.

"Recently, I went to a dinner, and a man who

may or may not be smart—I'll tell you later—suggested that I just share everything with you."

Traci looked at him oddly. "You share everything with me? I think that will take some time and some more trust," she said in a small voice.

Vincent gave her a sad smile.

"There is no one I trust more. The reason I don't tell you everything has actually nothing to do with this and everything to do with responsibility."

"I don't understand."

"It's true I have investigators go out and find out everything about everyone. What I never talk about is that keeping all those secrets is a big responsibility and can weigh on a person."

"Weigh on a person?"

"I have files on everyone in the business. Can you imagine what it's like to see someone about to do business with someone else, and you know that they have some secrets that might not make them a great choice? You have to make split decisions about whom you tell and whom you won't tell. More importantly, you'll have to be able to live with those decisions because they affect people's livelihoods of what they can and can't do.

"Maybe that guy was smarter than I gave him credit for. I never wanted you to think that the problem was about trust. You are my other half, and if I can't tell my other half everything, then whom can I tell?"

Tracy looked down into her lap, and the overwhelming sense of guilt weighed upon her.

"I have something to tell you, Vincent."

"Yes?"

"I've been going to fertility clinics and doctors to

make sure I'm okay if we want to have children. You know Sophia is my angel. I wanted her to have a brother or a sister, and I wanted to give you a family. I just wanted to make sure I was okay, and I meant to tell you but..."

"But you were scared."

Traci nodded. It didn't make sense not to confess it all now.

"Look at me, Traci"

She looked up, and instead of seeing an upset Vincent, she saw a remorseful one. "I'm so sorry that I made you feel like you couldn't just ask me. I guess we both have a lot to learn about trust. I am scared about having a family. What if they turn out like me?" he said in a quiet voice.

Traci reached out and cupped his chin.

"We can only hope for the best that they all turn out to be like you."

Vincent brought her hand to his lips and kissed the fingertips.

"You know I have problems trusting," he said.

"You're kind."

"I make everyone crazy with my need for order," he went on.

"You're intelligent and patient."

"I'm selfish, and I push people to their limits," he concluded.

"You're humble and give others the room to be all they can. I can go on all night doing this," Traci said with a smile.

"Are you sure?" Vincent asked.

"Sure of? Sure, that I love you? Yes. Sure, that you will make an absolutely amazing father? Yes.

Sure, that our family is going to be a bit odd? Without a doubt, and I can't wait."

"Neither can I. How about we go get hitched and then let Sophia pick a new home for her brother or sister? "Vincent asked, looking over Traci's hand.

Traci took her hand back.

"Vincent, who lets a five-year-old pick the house?"

"A father who can buy another one for her mom if she doesn't like that one?" Vincent asked.

Traci shook her head. "I love you, and yes, we can make it official, but we'll all choose a house," she said as she moved in closer and kissed him.

When they broke apart, he smiled at her. "It doesn't seem very efficient, but whatever you want to do."

"I love you, Vincent."

"I love you too, Traci…. Now can we go get married?"

"Ugh! We have to work on your delivery. Let's go!"

Kathy turned off her monitor and leaned back in her chair.

It had been way more meetings than she had thought she was going to attend initially. Her back hurt because she hadn't been able to get up and walk around. Her eyesight was blurry from looking at the screen, and she could tell she was getting the beginnings of a migraine slowly creeping up on her. When she tried to stand, she could feel the pain running up her back enough for her to whimper and have to sit back down.

"Kathy?" Reid said as he came into the room. "I wasn't sure if you were done or not."

Kathy looked at him and then looked away. "I'm done already," Kathy said. This day was just proof that she wasn't anywhere near as ready as she thought she was. While she was very productive today, she wasn't able to get to her end goal of meeting with people face-to-face.

"This was a long day in the conference and was way bigger than I thought it was going to be."

The only thing that Kathy could think about was that this was a bigger disappointment than she thought it was going to be. "I just want to go home."

"We're in New York. You don't want to go to one of these really fancy dinner places? I mean, I'm sure they have great stuff in the nay at home upstate, but we are in New York."

"I know you probably want to stay here to see if we can do the restaurant, and I won't have them put us in a private room. I get it. Maybe…"

"No, Kathy, which wasn't it. Ugh! I'm sorry if it's all been coming out like that."

"Reid, what's wrong?"

"Kathy, I just want to make your world right and take away any old pains you may have, and I think I tried so hard I didn't think about you."

"Stop, Reid. You're going to make me cry, and I'm not a pretty crier." Seeing Reid after the day she had, Kathy was ready to sink into a hole and not come out. She didn't know when the first tear started down her cheek, but she could feel the first splatter of her tears on her hands.

"Kathy, don't cry, please. I have been so slow. I thought I could fix it all with money, but it was just making a mess out of things. I hope you can forgive me."

Kathy was confused and only understood that her brother was pulling her in his arms and trying to apologize. For what? She wasn't clear.

"Of course, I can forgive you. You've only done the best by me. "

Reid leaned back, and then Kathy could really see him.

"Reid, you are starting to bruise. My goodness, what happened?"

Reid touched his face and shrugged.

"You had someone else come to see you for the day," Reid said.

"Reid, I hope you didn't bring Grayson or Vincent. The both of them are busy trying to get their own lives together."

"No, I didn't. I'm not completely slow, I think," Reid said.

"Well…" Kathy asked. "Who is here?"

Reid brightened. "He's not here now."

"Just step away from me now if the person you are about to say is Jack," Kathy said.

Reid stepped quickly back. Kathy dropped her head in her hands and tried to resolve her feelings. She was so mad at Reid for telling Jack and so thrilled that he came, even though Kathy knew he would not have approved of this plan. He loved her enough to support her even when he didn't like the idea.

"What can I do, Kathy?" Reid pleaded.

"Stay back. I'm still trying to decide if I should

give you a matching eye."

Reid threw his hands up.

"I don't get it. I'm wrong either way. If he were here, you'd be upset, and now he's not, and I'm still in trouble. Help me out."

"The issue here is you told him and didn't tell me. You should have told me that he was here. Then you have some bruising on you that suspiciously looks like you've been hit. I know that Jack wouldn't have been happy with me being here. He didn't want me to be here," Kathy rattled on.

"Oh, I know that," Reid said.

"Jack and I are in a relationship. I love you, Reid, but I don't need you to interfere."

"You two are in a relationship?"

Kathy looked at Reid, and she thought of the times Jack, and she had been together. Were they in a relationship? A smile came to Kathy's lips. Yes, they were in a relationship. Over the last few days, he had shown her that she could stay around Reid and also could have a relationship as well.

"Yes. Jack and I are an item. Now tell me, why did Jack hit you?"

Reid looked around the room and then sat down and sighed. "He called and tried to make an appointment with you. Then he found out that you weren't seeing anyone. I told him that you'd do better next time."

Kathy smiled and tried to imagine Jack becoming upset that Reid would put her through this again. There he was, protecting her again. It was one of the reasons she could go out with him. She knew she was safe with him no matter what.

"I'm going to have to talk to him when I see him. I can't you all having fights when you two disagree."

"Kathy, you don't sound very convicted. I also wanted to tell you that I'm sorry."

"Sorry?"

"I just wanted things to be normal. I guess I shouldn't say 'normal' either. I have been carrying around the thought that if I had just found you a little sooner, none of this would have been. I should have—a."

Kathy got up and pulled Reid into her arms. "You came right on time. I don't want you to think about anything else. You were the brother who didn't forget me. When I thought I had no one and no one cared, you came. You needed the time to get yourself together so that when you got home, we could stay together. It wasn't going to be a temporary thing. I can't tell you how grateful I am that you even kept looking for me and eventually found me. So, stop blaming yourself.

"I live an amazing life, and it is all a testament to you. So, there might be many things that we disagree on, but you found me at just the right time, and I need you not to feel bad about it."

Kathy felt Reid's hands tighten around her back.

"Okay, so I will work on it, but does that mean you are keeping Jack?"

Kathy laughed. "Oh, it definitely means that I am keeping Jack."

CHAPTER 18

"So, no girl in tow doesn't seem to bode well for the trip," Coram said over dinner. They had come to the local burger place. Jack hadn't eaten, and this seemed like a plan.

Jack wanted to take his mind off of things, and he thought calling his friend Coram would help. Certainly, he'd been gone long enough that they could talk about some things that were happening in the park. After hearing Coram s first question, Jack realized this was not going to go as planned.

"These things take time," Jack said.

"Do they? I mean, when we are selling something, and it's going well, do you think we have a lot of time to see how it's going? We see the sales like we've always known it was going to be a big hit."

Jack looked at Coram and shrugged. "Are you comparing Kathy and me to how we sell food in the trucks?"

"Yes, you know you have to find the right core items. That seems to be you and her. Then you have to find out how they fit together if they do. To date, she has been the only thing that has pulled you away from your truck. Well, not including the therapy in your garage. I think there must be some interest on both sides for that to happen.

"Lastly, you've been going out on dates. I mean, I haven't seen that in so long I thought you had taken some vows of celibacy and were about to become a monk," Coram said as he ate his fried nuggets.

"I don't think the analogy is relevant. Besides, I think I need to give her some space. She had a very trying day today, and I need to make sure I don't take away her independence by getting in her way," Jack said as he took a bite out of his burger.

Coram wiped his mouth on the back of his hand and sighed. "Wow, with that philosophy, you are going to be single for a long time."

Jack stopped eating and looked up at his friend. "What do you mean I'm going to be single for a long time?" Jack said.

"I mean just what I said. It seems like the only thing that you are waiting for is for her to decide everything that's going to be done in this relationship. The whole point is that you are supposed to be there for her when she needs you. And if you think waiting for her to tell you when to show up is a good idea, I'm here to tell you it doesn't work that way," Coram replied, tossing the rest of the nuggets.

"What makes you such an authority? You've been married forever."

"That, my friend, is exactly what makes me an authority. I have been married forever, but I will tell you, women do not change. The clothes may change, the fashion may change, a lot of other things may change, but at the end of the day, women do not change."

"I don't know if you should say that so loud. I'm sure there are plenty of women who would disagree with you."

"I bet you they wouldn't. There's not one woman here who doesn't want someone to love her and be there for her."

Jack stopped and thought about what Coram was saying. Had he read this all wrong? Was he really going to take advice from Coram?

"Okay, so what do you think I should do?"

Coram licked his fingers, and Jack knew he loved Kathy.

"That's easy, heartbreaker. You need to dazzle and wow your gal. You don't have to see her to let her know you think she's the world."

"Coram, she's filthy rich. What could I get her she couldn't get herself and probably a better quality of it?"

Coram leaned back in his seat and looked upon Jack in pity.

"Hey, don't give me the pitiful look," Jack said.

"What else can I do? You are not thinking about wooing a woman. I know the problem. You keep thinking you need to compete with every other rich guy that has ever met her. It's not true. Besides, I don't think it's the price of things that moves her. I mean, you took her on a picnic in the woods. This is not a woman who is concerned about cash or expensive gifts. Be thoughtful. Goodness, man. Just be yourself."

Jack repeated to himself the mantra "be me." It

couldn't be this easy and this hard all at the same time, could it? Jack didn't even remember what he'd eaten. The only thing that stood out from the meal was that he had to pay for it.

When he got home, he sat on the side of his bed and looked at his phone. Jack considered texting and then decided not to be a chicken. He called her.

"Hello?" Kathy said.

Jack felt like he hadn't heard her voice for the whole year. It was a balm to his soul.

"I was scared you weren't going to pick up my call. You know, with all those New York hunky guys waiting on you hand and foot and all."

Kathy laughed, and the sound vibrated through him.

"Those hunky guys have their hands out, and it's searching for my purse. Besides, I didn't even notice them. I was waiting for Prince Charming, but it seems he came and went. I was scared I had missed my moment."

"Missed your moment? I know Prince Charming. Every moment he has is yours."

"So, you know this was a dud," Kathy said in a low voice.

"No, it wasn't. It was a great first step, and you can take another one when you feel like it."

"Jack, I didn't see anyone."

"Kathy, you had to get to the room and set up. I was there, and I know that whole floor was a crush. You could have looked in there and decided it was a no-go, but you went forward."

"I think you are a bit jaded when it comes to my progress."

"No, I'm not. I'm a bit biased and jaded when it

comes to how strong, beautiful, and smart you are. But the progress? No."

"Jack, even when you didn't like this idea, you came. I want to do something that I think will work for us both."

"Hey, you can't!"

"Why not?"

"Because I have to do some distant wooing of you, so you know that I care for you and that you're the only one for me," Jack said emphatically.

He heard her laughing in the background and pulled the phone from his ear to make sure he still had her.

"I want you to know that I feel sufficiently wooed. Can we get to the good part?"

"That would be…"

"It would be the declaration of feelings for one another," Kathy said.

"Oh, well. Then I don't have to do anything because I've already told you that you are the one for me. I've laid open my heart because you are the only one who can heal it and make it whole."

"Oh, Jack. When you say it like that, then I guess I'm the holdout. I love you, Jack. I mean just in case you didn't know."

"Woman, you tell me this while you are miles away?"

"Actually, no."

"What?"

"I'm outside the door, and a very nice girl is waving at me from next door."

Jack ran to the door and saw a smiling Kathy standing outside. "I love you, Kathy.

"Good thing. Gas is expensive. I love you too, Jack Danvers."

Jack stepped out and grabbed Kathy in his arms before giving her a kiss on her forehead. He was going to have to tell Coram that he was right, after all.

EPILOGUE

*P*ortia hated gatecrashers, which was why she was standing in the cold with tall, dark and gorgeous.

"I need to see Grayson Chase," he said.

Portia smiled up at him.

"No, you want to see Grayson Chase. If you don't see him, you won't die."

The man stopped and looked her over.

"You are?" he asked with a little more than his fair share of disdain.

"I'm a friend of Grayson and Rose."

"Rose?"

"Rose is Grayson's wife She is having a baby shower now. You can see how we may not want some irate man to come barging in, saying he needs to see her husband talking about another woman. Optics, you know."

The man stopped and looked over Portia's shoulder at the door that she knew was still cracked. Portia had harbored some hope that she could get back inside the warm home. The hope was completely gone as she stood outside in the night air, looking at the face of determination on the stranger's face.

"So, do you want to tell me your name?" Portia asked.

"Franklin."

"Franklin. Is that like, you know, Prince or Madonna, where you only have one name, and I'm supposed to recognize it?" Portia asked as she crossed her arms over her chest. It was like the man had finally noticed her standing there.

"What are you, the bodyguard?" he asked, still not answering the question.

"I'm the one who answered the door, and if you'd like to get into this party or talk to Grayson, you're going to have to give me some answers first," Portia said pulling herself up to her full height which brought her midway to his chest.

"Well, then that would be the both of us because that's why I'm here too, for answers."

Portia looked at the man and thought to herself how come all of the crazy ones are gorgeous? It was so hard to find an attractive man who was over 6 feet. This one had that quality checked off the list, height was not an issue. Even with his brows furrowed and those little wrinkle lines showing up on his forehead, he still looked gorgeous.

"Okay Romeo, since it seems as though that you think that you are here for answers, why don't you ask me the questions and I'll see if I can get you on your way." For a moment, Portia didn't think he was going to take the bait, but then he took a step back, let out a deep breath, and then fired away.

"A couple of months ago, my sister came by, and she left a message saying she had gotten an acting gig."

"Congratulations, and I'm listening."

"She left me a message saying that she was coming here to Inheritance Bay and that she was going to meet up with someone by the name of Grayson Chase. Or Chance?

" You had it right the first time."

"Anyway, she came, and then she never called me back. It's true my sister can run off and do things on her own, and she is indeed a grown woman, but we always keep in touch."

Portia felt something melt in her heart to hear him talk about his sister. She wondered if she had anybody who would go ahead and inconvenience themselves and come looking for her. She shook her head. This wasn't about her. It was about Grayson and Rose.

"So, your sister was an actress, and supposedly she had a job working with Grayson.?"

"That's what the message said. Listen, I'm not here to crash a party.

"But you did." Portia interrupted.

"Or to ruin anything for anyone. I'm just looking for my sister."

Portia looked at tall, dark, and handsome one more time.

"Listen to me. I'm going to get you in the party so you will see your sister isn't there. We'll pull Grayson to the side to ask him what he remembers. When he's done, I'm sure it will all be clear on what happened."

Franklin nodded and then went to the door.

"Whoa, soldier, where are you going?"

"Inside?" Franklin said as he began to walk by Portia.

"No, gorgeous, we are going in together," she said slowly as if he were slow to understand.

"Together?" he mimicked, confused.

"Yes, together. This is a private affair. If you just show up, you will just be shown out."

Clearly, frustrated, Franklin looked at Portia.

"So, what do you suggest?"

Portia held out her hand.

"You can take my hand, and we go in together, or I call out that you're a stranger and they take you away to the jail that I assure you isn't very comfy in this town because almost no one goes to. It's your choice, gorgeous."